HER GUARDIAN ANGEL WAS PUSHED

HEART
BORN

Thank You!

BS:

TERRY MAGGERT

HEARTBORN

First published in USA in 2016 by

Terry Maggert

Portland

Tennessee

Copyright © Terry Maggert 2016

Formatted by CyberWitch Press LLC

ACKNOWLEDGMENTS

No author ever truly exists in a bubble, although some may hope for such a disconnected state of being. I am not one of those people. In fact, this book would not *be* without the considerable efforts of an enormous array of people, all of whom inspired or shamed me to write more, better, and with a greater degree of respect for the characters than ever before.

My friend Staci Hart was, and is, made of spun gold. She not only created this stunning cover art, she encouraged me with both her own excellence and her humor. If you think snorting like a piglet isn't good for one's soul, I suggest you try it.

My friend March McCarron swooped in and created the map of Sliver and its environs, doing so while living somewhere named "Korea". Since our time difference was approximately two and a half days, I'm stunned at what she was able to create with only the barest of details. So, thanks, March — be you in the future or past right now.

Thanks to my friend Brad, who patiently listened to me describe a book that would have been an impossibility a decade earlier. You know it.

There are a host of other people who make me a better writer, but to my bride Missy goes the glory. She helps in many ways, big and small, and without her, the kid, and the home base from which I launch my creative forays — this book doesn't happen.

As always, any errors within are my own. I'll do better next time. Promise.

Terry Maggert,
June 30, 2016

This book is dedicated to my son Teddy,
who thinks that compromise is for the weak.

Northern
Ramparts
Western
Frontier
Eastern
Reaches
House
Windhook
Sliver
Rogue
Armies
Southern
Wilds

CHAPTER ONE:

The Leap

*T*he relentless wind cooled his skin as he mustered the courage to jump. It was a long way to fall, and he'd been poised on the edge for nearly an hour. It wasn't fear that kept him rooted to the spot, but the effort of reaching through time to see what consequences his action might bring. To think of leaving was akin to dropping a boulder in the pool of his own history; there was no way to foresee what the ripples might cause. Or the waves, since this would make waves, not ripples. It was all an undiscovered thing.

No one had done what he meant to do; at least not in the memory of his House.

Under the points of his boots, featureless mist curled away to reveal an enticing glimpse of color and life so unlike his own home. *Gray*, he thought. *I am so very tired of all the gray in these clouds.* The longer he looked at the myriad of colors below, the more acute his hunger to *see* what mysteries rolled beneath him, unknown and vibrant. The land looked like a fairy tale made real, its hills and rivers gleaming like a promise in the early morning light. The sheer distance and appeal of it all clutched at his chest like a physical thing, making him cover his heart. His body fizzed with excitement and fear, and he liked it.

"You won't go, you know." His brother's voice was bored to the point of insolence, a tone he'd perfected from years of practice. Like others who kept their face an impassable mask, he'd lost much of the joy in his life, if ever he knew it. Brother Garrick appeared from the sullen gray mist that hid the secret columns and towers of their home. Walking toward Keiron, a smile quirked at the cruel lips, so unlike his own. "We've already been to the edge of the scrying pool. You won't go. It is known to *us*." A look flickered across the impassive face, something ugly and hot. His control was slipping. That was new, as was his belief that he was equal to their parents. Or older siblings, at that.

"Yes. I will." Keiron's voice sounded small in the silence. Even the wind died out of respect for what he was about to say, and if his resolve held, what he would then do.

A sad shake of the perfect head said that was a lie. Garrick was beautiful to the point of distraction. His pupils were nearly colorless in a face framed with fine blonde hair that called sunlight to mind, so different from his brother. Garrick was light, while Keiron was dark, with skin golden from the sun and eyes the black of a starless night. A long, aquiline nose gave him a regal quality that Garrick, for all his perfection, could not possess. His hair was curled and ebony to the point of being liquid, a black mass that he pushed back with irritation at Garrick's verbal assault. Keiron was lean and tall, and in the stages of bloom where men first leave boyhood behind when they are no longer concerned with a young man's things.

Garrick spoke again, substituting arrogance for wisdom. "No. There is no escaping that which has passed. Even if you were to—"

A swift cut of Keiron's hand broke the thought. His brother looked shocked, then amused, and then angry.

He didn't like being spoken to that way. "I can, and I will. I know how to shift the light of days, and I know *when* to do it, too."

"Really? A secret of that size, and you, a minor son, have figured it out? Do tell, fledgling." He loved using Keiron's youth as an insult, even though he was barely a year older.

"If you paid attention to anything other than yourself, you'd know that there is logic behind the Moondivers. There have been others, you know." A hint of smugness colored Keiron's defense, but his brother had it coming.

The reaction was volcanic.

Real anger spat forth from Garrick now, contorting his features into something crude and ugly. It was, Keiron thought, the first honest thing he'd seen of his brother in all these years. It was the face of fear and rage, and he knew why. This entire outburst was about power, or the lack of it. To control time was the province of elders, not some child who thought that he could move the forces of worlds to right a wrong. It was arrogance of a kind unlike anything he'd ever embraced, and his brother's hate for him grew by the second because he knew that for all his perfection, the younger of them was more pure. The elder boy was ambition personified, but without courage and purity he would never control the clocks. For that matter, Garrick would not even control himself, a fact that dawned on him as he sputtered with rage.

Keiron squared his feet and repeated his intentions like a prayer. "The days will bend for me. I can feel it, and your anger will not change the truth." His words rang with a kind of surety that made his legs shake, if only briefly.

It was something Garrick would say, and for that he was frightened and proud, since unlike his brother, Kieron meant every word of it and aimed to see it through.

In two long strides, his brother came close enough that he could smell the wind herbs on his breath. They were sour with hate, just like the expression contorting his face. "She's already dead."

Keiron went rigid, but fought mightily to gain control of the anger that bloomed in his chest. Heat spread like sunlight, and he took three long breaths to contain his next words. "She is now, but she won't be when I get there. I told you. I can do it."

"You think falling through time and distance can save her? Landing in that mud-spattered wallow that they crawl about in like feral swine? You don't even know *why* they were driven from the land, let alone if death awaits you. What about *you*? Who can save you?" His brother barked with laughter, a short noise of jealousy and fear. "What if she doesn't want to be saved? You're a child. A favored pet who is loved because of his youth. You're nothing but an amusement to this family."

The wind blew harder as spots filled Keiron's vision. He could not lose control, not now. He worked his jaw to let the words out. The sounds followed each other, chastened by the force of his will. "I have watched. I have learned. And I tell you, I am going, and she is worth saving."

Garrick shrugged as the boredom returned to his face, now a mask of beautiful disinterest. "You *actually* care about them, don't you? Those things down there? Those glorified cattle? Do you think they're even *capable* of understanding us? We are not the benign, soft creatures that have been reshaped by their pitiful legends. We were born for war, not love. We are made to hurt, not heal." He shook his head with a mocking grin. "You've always been weak, but this is beyond anything the family expected. It's practically — "

"It's decent, that's the word you're looking for." Keiron's voice was like iron, despite a small quiver at the end of his words. His jaw set again, and for an instant Garrick saw their grandfather's stern profile there, lurking like a boulder under the surface of a still pool.

"You're not even worth saving, let alone one of *them*." Garrick's eyes flicked down to the vista that unspooled under their feet, or perhaps it was above. It was difficult to tell with the curving horizon and shifting light. Part of what he saw was green, unlike their home. There were blue rivers, brown and green fields, and stony places worn by wind and weather. It was alien, but enticing. He let a woven cord of animal hide fall into his hand. On either end, a heavy molar prized from the jaw of a Windbeast acted as a weight. The teeth were well worn, and tied in with strands of fine leather. It had been a mature beast, killed to make things that the people of the wind needed. Like teeth. And rope.

"Then I belong with them, don't I?" Keiron's question was rhetorical.

Again, Garrick shrugged, this time with one shoulder. His lips peeled back to reveal perfect teeth, but there was no kindness in the gesture. "Fine, but you'll need to know something first." The cord spun outward from Garrick's hand in a blur, spinning around Keiron's wings with brutal efficiency. The weight of the heavy teeth spun the strand tight to bind him, flightless, as Garrick drew his sword and cut downward in a wicked blow that sent Keiron's wings spinning away into the clouds below.

Paralyzed by pain and betrayal, Keiron stood swaying as Garrick stepped calmly forward, placing both hands on his brother and pushing him into a chaotic tumble from the ledge of House Windhook. Spatters of blood swept up and away in the swirling winds, the last sign of a boy who had been bound, and cut, and sent into the sky in less time than he had to register the sensation of being flightless and wounded.

Keiron's stomach raged upward as glare and shadow coursed around him in a never-ending circle of dizzying light, and he began the long, cold fall through layers of sky and time that tore the scream from his throat even as it began.

From above, he heard Garrick's last words, mocking and fat with poisonous joy. "Let us see if you can truly fly."

CHAPTER TWO:

Saturday

*E*ven though she'd only been there for a few hours, Livvy knew some important numbers. It was part of her nature to do so because of her condition. Her lips were starting to get dry, which meant that in a few minutes she'd be thirsty, and since she couldn't have a drink at her desk, that meant she was faced with three choices. She sighed, a small noise made smaller by her natural desire to remain invisible when she was in new surroundings. She was a polite, pretty girl, and grand, emotional gestures weren't her style. She kept her dark brown hair pulled down over one eye; or at least she did when she wasn't wearing glasses. Livvy had a heart-shaped face and eyes like caramels that swam amongst a sea of freckles that faded closer to her hairline, just like the stars do when morning begins. She was pale and fragile, and not too tall but not too short. In her own eyes she fell somewhere in the middle, although her parents had always said she was a beauty of legend if she would only let herself shine.

Livvy looked around meekly and began to count. It

was early afternoon, but she was already tired and a little bit sore, and wondering how long the day would be. It was a terrible way to live, especially for a girl who wanted more than anything to simply draw a single, clean, deep breath and laugh without fear of what came after a normal moment of joy.

It was forty-two steps to the bathroom on her right, and another three steps past that to the water fountain. That meant forty-five in total, which she knew would mean taking at least one break in which she put a hand against the wall and pretended to look interested at something nearby. The bland walls weren't worth a second look, nor were the aggressively neutral prints that peppered her pathways. The art seemed to consist of two distinct kinds: faded flowers done in watercolor, and non-specific buildings that might have been important had she known their context. As it was, not one picture hanging on the wall looked like anything other than a faded echo, so she would, after becoming winded, have to peer at them with exaggerated interest while the rest of the world walked by with strong hearts and none of her worries.

She was, in her own way, an excellent actress, cultivating an outward image of casual uncaring as her heart slowed and her lungs filled once again to capacity. While she was doing so, someone would inevitably come by and want to talk, and that meant that she'd be hiding the fact that her chest felt like a heaving bellows under the forced calm of her outward appearance. If no one bothered her, she could recover her breath in a minute or two and move on, but it would be slowly, like a ship that plunged through waves at a reduced but dignified speed. She licked her lips again, thinking, because that was what Livvy did. She thought. She considered. Sometimes, on days *not* like today, she planned. She wasn't sure she *needed* a drink, but she was already getting thirsty, so the second option came into play like an unwelcome relative at dinner. She could go left, but hesitated.

Fifty-eight steps to the left was the breakroom, or what passed for a breakroom on her floor. There were chairs, and she could get something out of the fridge, but the distance was great enough that she'd be obliged to take a second break from walking, probably mere feet from the door. That meant a longer, more-tiring trip with double the chances of being forced to talk while fiercely trying to reclaim her wind. But, she had something sweet to drink, and it would be ice cold and a lot better than water, if she was honest.

The third option was to wait until break time, but that wouldn't work. The air was cool and dry to protect the books, and she'd more or less made her mind up that waiting that long would leave her fidgeting and irritable.

So, she stood.

With an apologetic look around in case anyone was watching, she took a careful step away from her desk, pushed the chair in, and began to walk in a manner that was more dignified than scared. Because it was afternoon and she was tired, her breath began to come in shorter gasps after only fifteen steps. She'd hoped for twenty-three, and the onset of her discomfort scared her a little more than it had on her last trip, just before lunch. Maybe she was fading a bit. It *had* been a full day, and her first on a new job. A whirlwind, really, if you compared this day to so many others in her seventeen years of life.

She put a hand out, noticing that at least for a moment,

she was alone. With eyes closed, she let the spaces of her mind fill with the *lup lup lup* of her heart as it raced ahead, trying to keep her standing. Thankfully, she hadn't fainted today, but it could happen. Livvy collected bruises like other girls claimed boyfriends. Both could hurt. Until now, Livvy had been alone, kept apart from boys like some exotic creature who would turn to dust under their attentions. In her own way, she thought it worse than a broken heart; the kind that was a part of her everyday life, not just something that you could get through with a good cry and then move on. There was no running from her kind of broken heart, with its wild pacing and erratic sounds.

One more step now, Liv. You got this. In her head, she sounded cheerful instead of scared. She pulled her dress down, wondering yet again just how cold the air conditioning could be, then started off at a careful pace. She wanted something sweet, so it was breakroom or bust. If she had to take five stops to catch her breath, it wouldn't matter. It was her first day, and there had to be some good in it. If it came in the form of chocolate, all the better.

"Away from your desk again, Livvy?" The voice drifted over her shoulder, scaring her just enough that she twitched. *Lup Lup Lup* went her heart, ticking upward in a tiny rebellion of fear. After a long breath, she turned to see Miss Henatis standing, finger pointed like an accusation in her general direction. She towered over Livvy, a woman of perhaps fifty years with a halo of black curls and a severe face. Her dark eyes were always looking *over* Livvy's head, like she wasn't good enough to be recognized.

Livvy looked down, not sure what to say. Miss Henatis was the library director, and wore a gray suit cut so primly that it covered her knees. She wore dark makeup that seemed to sculpt her already sharp features into something hungry. Livvy was scared of her at an instinctive level, but she was respectful.

"Y—yes, Miss Henatis. I need a drink." Livvy looked around, as if the unseen winds of the air conditioning could be made to show themselves. "I think it's the air in here."

Miss Henatis sniffed. It was patronizing and distant. "As I explained during your orientation, we can't have untreated air in here. You understand, of course." She waved away any protests, but there were none. When she saw Livvy was still quiet, she looked toward the breakroom. "If you *must*, then go. But don't think for a moment that your condition precludes you from obeying the rules of the library. You're not a volunteer, Livvy, and that means that you'll be kept to the same standards as I am, or any other person with a desk. We must set an example of the utmost dedication and care for this place." She looked around with something like pride, but it looked uncomfortable on her features.

Livvy's hand went to her chest without thinking, and she nodded, understanding. Yes, things were different for her, but not because she was lazy. With a final glare of admonition, Miss Henatis muttered a terse goodbye before stalking off to find someone else to harass.

Livvy stood, just breathing. There were thirty-six steps ahead of her, and the carpeted flooring yawned away like a distant valley. The bookshelves loomed like mountains, and in a second she felt small, and tired, and very, very thirsty. Her fingers ran over the line up her chest, feeling the incomplete rhythm of her traitorous heart beating away at its losing game. She would not cry. Not now. So she tucked that fear and anger away at her station in life because standing in the library weeping like a little kid wouldn't do anything to fix her. There was nothing that could make her whole.

Livvy was unique, but that didn't always mean better. For of all the girls who had ever been born, she was the only one who lived, and breathed, and dreamed while only having half of her heart. A strong, good half, but still — only a part. She was a miracle, but right then she didn't feel like one.

And I need that half to take me to the breakroom, now. She stepped forward, the cool air blowing across her. She would make it.

Half had been good enough until now. And it would be good enough until she quit trying, and that wasn't ever going to happen.

CHAPTER THREE:

House Windhook

*D*id you feel it?" Saiinov asked his wife, who sat overlooking the scrying pool, her face a mask of cultivated strength. He was a handsome, angular man with a face made of masculine planes under eyes that glittered with dark intensity. His hair, nearly black, was cut short in the way of swordsmen, who left nothing to chance in their brutal occupation. He smiled often, but most frequently when looking at his wife or children. Despite his position of power, Saiinov's greatest glory was his family, and his fond looks revealed a kindness hidden under the guise of a man who was at the absolute peak of his skill as a Skywatcher.

"Yes, it's happened. He's gone." Vasa was a brave woman of rare intellect, but the departure of her youngest child left shadows dancing under the pretense of impassive control. She was lithe, with long honey hair and eyes that ranged from blue to gray depending on the skies. Her lips were full, and kind, often pulled upward in a look of thoughtful mirth. Vasa wore her joy outside for all to see, and it kept her luminous with beauty well into her middle years. Her expression grew younger still when she spoke of her children, especially Keiron. His birth set him apart from all others, lending him a special status among the family, although to admit such a thing was beneath Vasa's loving sensibilities.

He was her baby, in some ways. Saiinov certainly thought of him that way, although their opinions varied at to Keiron's ultimate purpose in life.

She trailed two fingers through the water of the pool. Twin ripples tracked outward to rebound from the far edges, their power diminishing only slightly with the distance. Soon, the pool would fall quiet again, but not before she saw Keiron landing in a field of cut stalks and tattered snow. It looked like late winter, that time when the hopeless see nothing but gray. In truth, they're right, as the darkest months are always longest. Saiinov watched over her bare shoulder, the flesh stippled with a chill or fear; he couldn't be certain which, and respected her too much to ask for clarification. She wore a simple robe of the Scholar, which was her calling, but on her it became something living. Each curve of her body was a testament to the power and daring she used to assure their family's success. That made what had just happened all the more difficult, and he knew it. His touch was light, but filled with care. She was mother, and teacher, and protector. He was curator, and hunter, and master over the winds, and in that moment there was nothing that either of them could do for their youngest child, who had fallen through the skies to save a girl with a connection to House Windhook that only they could understand.

"How long do you think we have before the Crescent Council will know?" she asked.

It was a reasonable question. Keiron would be missed, sooner or later. It might be a friend, although the boy had few. It might be a new routine, or a missed detail, but someday soon his presence would be missed, and shortly after that the council would know. Then, things would get interesting.

"A week, perhaps? I think that we should hope for ten days, but plan for seven." Saiinov was practical to a fault in times like this. He had to be. As a man who chased demons through the clouds, he could afford little in the way of dreams, because dreams led to mistakes. In his chosen pursuits, you were only allowed one such error, and then your House would be carving your name on the Columns of the Lost.

"Seven, then. I think that feels right." There were tears in her eyes. She hoped against everything that their son would be brave and bold. They knew he was pure; of that there could be no doubt.

Among their six children, only Keiron had a default setting of kindness. Garrick, the closest to him, was the least likeable of all, and yet Keiron had always managed to share love and compassion with his only brother. Their four sisters were all older, and thus occupied with different things. As with all eldest children, Prista had become a Scholar, like her mother. She dove into the past, seeking the meanings of glyphs so old that their very shape had been forgotten, and nearly lost to the depths of time. The mists were unkind to items of the distant peoples who had come before House Windhook and her allies, and Prista's ability was solidly in the class of the great masters. To master one's future, it was necessary to understand the past.

Habira was second eldest and a born warrior. Even as

a child, she'd shown no fear of the winds and heights, choosing her path as a Skywatcher on the earliest date that she could declare. She was bold, and brash, and utterly calm in the face of danger. Of all their children, it was Habira to whom they could trust their lives, because her martial skills were surpassed only by those of her father.

The twins, Banu and Vesta, shared everything except men. Their interests had clarified to a diamond focus upon entering their second round of Seeking; it was there that they found a destiny for their inquisitive minds and patient hands. They were master Watershapers, whose gifts at molding deep cloud banks of immense power were known across the breadth of the empire. Every time Saiinov heard the distant roll of thunder, he wondered if his daughters had been the source of such wondrous storms, and his heart fairly sang with pride as it did for all of his children. Even vain, beautiful Garrick was an untapped well of power. Vasa declared that when Garrick could harness his pride, he would then find the heart of a Windshaper beating in his chest. But he was young, and not yet seasoned enough to let emotion fall to the wayside when talent wished to muscle forth.

It was silent in their home, save the distant whisper of breezes that had other places to go. They sat next to each other, hand in hand, wondering what changes were in store for the family. Or the empire, for that matter, because House Windhook was no minor polity to be discounted should there be a catastrophe. The ocean of sky was mankind's last refuge, and it was houses like theirs that made life — civilization, even — possible. They both looked through their home, with walls of whirling shapes and the delicacy of an ancient shell, tossed onto the sands of a beach that was lost forever to humanity. Everything around them spoke of a place where water and sky grew together, life taking cues from memories that were so distant as to be legends. After long moments of companionable quiet, Vasa grew somber as the enormity of their path began to take hold in the recesses of her awareness. Then she saw Saiinov's lips moving, silently, and knew that their histories were being made regardless of her desires. Angels would move forward from their comfortable roost, or they would die as a people. There was nowhere in which to be safe, not if they wanted to be free.

As one, they cast prayers to the winds, watching as the words were carried up, then down, and hoping that in the end of it all the words would find their son. It was all they could do for the moment, and that had to be enough.

CHAPTER FOUR:

Monday

*L*ibraries open at a civilized hour. That was one of the reasons Livvy quickly decided that her new job was a good thing, despite the looming menace of Miss Henatis. Everything about the head librarian was intimidating, right down to when she corrected Livvy for pronouncing her name wrong. With a half-sneer, the tall, severe woman had explained her name was pronounced *Terezza*, not Teresa, like the unwashed masses, but Livvy was to address her only as Miss Henatis, since the library was a professional atmosphere and not some wild scene of casual familiarity.

So, at 9:55 in the dull, overcast morning, Livvy sat at her desk after taking several breaks to catch her breath following the long walk into the building, past the lower floor, and out of the elevator, where she suffered a tense, cloistered ride with several people who never looked up from their phones except to grimace at the lack of a good signal. Once she reached her desk, she quickly assessed the condition of her workspace before sitting down on her chair with a muffled *whoosh*. The cushion was welcoming, her pens were in order, and Livvy Foster began her second day as the assistant Answer Desk Librarian (2nd Floor).

"Hiya."

The light smell of hand sanitizer wafted toward her as she turned to see a slender young man in a perfectly crisp blue shirt drop into the seat next to her. He wiped his hands in a practiced motion, flicking his fingers with a final gesture of satisfaction. Apparently, germs were a sworn enemy. His smile was brilliant, and she found herself responding in kind with something more like a dopey grin.

"Dozer. Nice to meetcha." Before she could react, he was plucking at her shirt with busy fingers, smoothing an imaginary wrinkle with a light touch. "Before you say anything, we're totally gonna be besties, and yes, I know what you're thinking."

"You do?" Livvy asked, overwhelmed with his on-slaught of charm. She shook her head to clear it, but he just grinned even more.

"Yes. It's part of my job as your New Best Friend. You're asking a lot of things right now, but in your head, so let me help." He held up a finger and winked. "Item one. *How* am I so good looking?"

Livvy burst out laughing, then had to place a hand over her heart as the stitch began to build in her side. She didn't care. It felt good to laugh that way, and she took little sips of air while waving that he should continue. He didn't pay her breathing any mind, so neither did she, reveling in the normalcy of a shared joke with someone new. It felt good to forget, if only for a moment. That was a good start if they were going to be friends. Besties, according to Dozer.

"You don't look like a Dozer."

He was impeccably dressed in blue, and his dark blonde hair was styled to sweep up off his forehead. Cheerful blue eyes crinkled at her as he smiled, and his teeth were small, white, and even. She held out a hand, and he took it. His grip was delicate and caring, like he sensed her condition but was too kind to mention it. It was a small thing, but it made tears threaten the corners of her eyes. She smiled harder to blink them away.

"Well, don't let this flawless appearance confuse you." His sniff was so perfectly arrogant that she felt like cheering. He smiled at her again, then slid his own chair so that he faced her at a ninety-degree angle. "Item two, and this is important, so pay attention." When he saw her nod, he pointed out at the rows of desks, and books, and all the things that made the library into a sort of living thing. "I know all about this place, and more importantly, I know everyone who comes in here. I can tell you who's happy, or sad, or drunk, or homeless, or fighting with their wife or husband. I know why they're here, and I know if they're leaving and never coming back."

Livvy made appropriate cooing noises at this declaration, but they weren't polite. She meant it.

Dozer cocked his head and raised a brow, looking like the picture of a screen idol from a time long ago. "Stick with me and I'll show you the ropes, kid."

Her laugh bubbled again, free and easy. "We *are* going to be besties, I think." A blush colored her cheeks at her brashness; it wasn't like her to be that direct and open. She was steady, and loyal, and a lot of other things that people said when they didn't want to call you only sort of pretty, but Dozer was so gallant that she had to respond in kind.

He leaned in, conspiracy on his mind. "See the big guy over there?" Pointing with his chin, he directed her eyes over to one of the tables where the regulars sat. There were a stalwart few who came in every day. Their pecking order was written in stone, as if the chairs were ordained by a higher power.

"The man with the mustache?" she asked.

He was a big, solid guy with a shock of white hair and deeply tanned skin. His shoulders bulged with muscle, even though he had to be pushing sixty years of age. There were dark blue tattoos on both forearms, and his smile was lopsided and kind.

"Mmm-hmm. That's Sailor Mark. He's a good one. Sort of worked as a plumber all his life, and now he spends his days here. He's a really nice guy, tells a lot of great stories. You'll meet him, I'm sure." Dozer selected his next target — a slender, harried looking woman with frizzy hair pulled back in a bun. She had sad brown eyes and coffee-colored skin, and she moved between the tables to her seat with an economy of motion and certainty that Livvy found fascinating.

"What does she like to read?" Lizzy looked thoughtful, watching the woman flit about like a hummingbird. The question surprised her new friend, who put a hand on his chin to think before answering. She liked that he gave her words consideration. It was a sign that she was being seen and valued. Her blush returned, but hidden from his sight due to his concentration on the scene before them.

"Miss Willie?" He watched the woman settle at a table, but only after a great deal of fuss in which she adjusted her chair, her book, her feet, and then her chair once again in a series of tiny scooting motions until she had everything *just so*. "Mostly adventure novels, and some old-fashioned romances. She's kind of sappy that way. I asked her about, like, a billion new books and she said she didn't have time for them. She just likes to relax, I think, but she doesn't really know how. Sometimes I see her going over the same boring old things over and over. But she's quiet and friendly, so—" He shrugged to indicate his powerlessness over such plodding book choices.

"What about, umm, the guy with the ponytail?" She watched the man tapping his fingers to an unknown beat as he flipped listlessly through a magazine about science and cars, but from Livvy's standpoint it seemed to have an awful lot of women in bikinis.

"Oh! Right, that's Drum Circle Danny, or just Danny." Dozer's eyes glimmered with mischief. "He can't help drumming on stuff, so don't tease him about it."

"I wouldn't dare." Livvy meant it. He looked kind of crunchy and harmless, like an intellectual who'd gone back to nature.

"He comes in first, usually. Sometimes he's here up to an hour before the others show up. Gets his stuff set up, but always quietly. I like him. He loves books about the ocean. I think he has a lot of stress in his life, and reading about whales or whatever lets him calm down." Dozer's one shoulder shrug was just enough; Danny was okay, too. That was the message Livvy got.

"How many are there? Regulars, I mean?" She counted the table and booths. There was room for at least two dozen people in this little nook alone.

Dozer thought it over, then started counting on his fingers. "Depends on what's happening. We have special events here, sometimes. On a busy day we might get ten or twelve of them. It's always a moving group, sort of like a school of fish. I can count them when they're still, but they move around. . ." He brightened. "What are you doing for lunch?"

"Nothing, why?" She hadn't thought that far ahead.

"You are now. I'm going to introduce you to the wonder of Frankly, Frank's. He's down on the plaza, right by all those benches." At her hesitation, Dozer added, "My treat. And honey, I know."

Tears pricked her eyes. He was so nice, and she didn't want to ruin the feeling of having someone think about her kindly. "I want to, I mean, I do, but —"

"Don't worry." Dozer took her hand gently, but not like she might break. Even sitting down, he was taller than Livvy. "And I mean: Do. Not. Worry. I know all about your, ahh —" He pointed at her chest, and spots of color bloomed on her cheeks again, but this time it was some-thing like shame. "Anyway, I know all about it, and we can go nice and slow down to the plaza, okay?"

Livvy knew right there and then; Dozer, the exotic, funny boy sitting next to her was going to be a true friend.

CHAPTER FIVE:

Landing

*G*reen. That was the first sign that Keiron was somewhere and somewhen else. The drab grays of home were gone, replaced by a vibrant, lush promise of springtime. Everything in his vision was on the cusp of exploding into action as the days grew longer, warmer, and alive. With exaggerated delicacy, he moved his head slowly, like it was full of water because the fall had been long and his push backward into the light of days left him sore and muzzy. Whatever he'd expected, it hadn't been a body filled with dull aches and the promise of bruises to come.

"Maybe I'll just sit here until my head is clear." The wind freshened with a hint of rain, squelching the idea of inactivity. In stages, he dragged himself painfully upright, wondering for the first time why he hadn't merely glided all the way to his landing. As he rose, his arms began to pinwheel in a wild gyration, ending only when he pitched face forward into the moist grass with an inelegant thud.

The only time he'd ever fallen in his entire life had been when he was a child, before he learned how to open —

His wings were gone. A searing jolt of fear raged through him, spiking into every corner of his body and ending in the most delicate place it could.

His mind.

He shook, breath coming in ragged gasps while reaching desperately over each shoulder to find nothing but empty air. He was stripped, defenseless, and maimed.

He was broken. He was *ordinary*.

And ordinary was not good enough to save her.

Only twice in his life had stories of the wingless come to him; in each case, the piteous creature had been a criminal who the council banished for a shadowy reason so heinous it was kept from the children. But this — his hands waved in a weak rhythm as if they too could not believe his condition. He was, what, exactly? Wingless? No, that could not be, as he'd committed no crime. Garrick, his brother and apparent rival, had pushed him from House Windhook. Keiron's thoughts and intentions were far from criminal, and could be no reason for banishment, let alone stealing his wings.

Still, he sat, pained with the understanding that this was truly a one-way trip. His cause had gone from noble to permanent, and he knew that the vistas of House Windhook were now little more than a memory.

He would save her or die. It was simple as that.

In fact, he thought of countless variables in which he could save her and *still* die, but he forced those from his mind by will alone, raising himself on swooning knees and elbows as he tried to stand again.

This time he was successful, albeit uncertain of how long it would be before he could take a step. The ground swayed like a runaway cloud bank, mindless of his lack of balance and lending an aura of chaos to the simple act of looking out over the horizon.

But what a horizon! It was *alive*. There were budding trees, two rivers that met far ahead, and a riot of greens that seemed to challenge everything he had ever known about what it meant to be lush. Closing his eyes, he waited until the whirling sensation left him, and only then did he unclench his hands and truly drink in the landscape. It was magnificent, and the ground was soft to the touch of his boots. He recalled the page from a pilfered book he read prior to taking the fall; in it, it was known that all waters ran to the sea, a body of water so unimaginably large that Keiron thought it most likely a wild legend and nothing more. There was a river close enough that he could smell the water, so he pointed himself toward it and took the first of his ginger steps.

Then he took a second, and a third.

In between breaks necessitated by the return of his dizziness, he made his careful way to the riverbank. The flow, while broad and steady, was gentle enough that he could approach the water directly. Keiron feared no water, save the possibility of a sea, so he crouched for a moment to examine the broad, slow ribbon that passed by in a lazy current. The water was somewhere between green and brown, rich with earthy scents, and flecked with parts of things that Keiron was certain had, at one time, been living trees.

It was utterly magical, and it paid him no mind; unlike a storm, which could reach out to the inquisitive and snuff their curiosity with a single, well-placed bolt of lightning. Even his sisters, Banu and Vesta, would be daunted by the sight of so much untamed water running where it wished, with no guidance from a Watershaper. He wasn't even certain they were capable of altering something this natural. They were powerful, but this was a massive, undisciplined feature that would not take kindly to meddling. Even as he concluded this, a tree — yes, he was certain it had been one — rolled over in the river, exposing a claw-like base of battered roots. The wood was smooth and bleached, like the bones of a cloudbeast left to polish in the elements before being used as a decorative gate for some proud House. All around him, the world busied itself with concerns other than him, and for once in his life, he was thankful.

"The book says that water will flow to a sea. Cities are on the banks of the rivers, usually, and that's where I may find her." He shrugged to himself, turned downstream, and began to walk toward the unseen depository of the water. He picked his steps carefully, only daring to speed up after he'd passed one-hundred paces without any disquiet in his balance. It wouldn't do to fall into a river when he was this close to his goal. Despite not having nearly the skills of his sisters, he drew a small prayer in the water, watching the words whisked away downstream to where she would be waiting.

Keiron wondered if she would be there when the simple words swept by, their message of hope and love visible only to her. If not, he could send another. He had many prayers to send, and all of the time he'd created by the arc of his dive.

For now, he could be patient. He only hoped that she could, too.

CHAPTER SIX:

Messenger

*S*aiinov heard the messenger's bold call before the wingshadow dimmed the light streaming into his workroom. They always flew with such martial import-ance, never caring for whose light they stole, or if they gave offense by shouting their arrival before even folding a single feather. Since messengers were considered an extension of the Crescent Council, they often acted with complete impunity, knowing that their behavior would only bolster the intimidation on which they seemed to thrive.

House Windhook was not impressed.

Vasa's footsteps were quick and light; there was no worry in her motion, only decisive action. "Flyer is here, bearing a shell." She assessed her husband's body language and nodded, aware that he knew of the arrival and was already in motion.

Saiinov pulled his tunic closed and fastened the silver loops that held it in place over the wide expanse of his chest. He was a lean, angular man with no excess, and the tunic matched his body like a second skin. The fabric danced in brilliant tones of silver and blue—two colors that bordered on heresy in the unwavering, plain uniforms of the upper Houses, who nearly always favored shades found in the clouds. Vasa quirked a brow in approval, and for an untold time Saiinov admired the rare beauty of his wife. They were more than a matched pair; they were extensions of each other in all things. The initial political gambit by an unseen envoy would be met with a unified front, and nothing less.

Together, they strode from his private space, their heels allowed to click with latent menace on the wide floor of the main hall. Their home matched its purpose based on the will and magical needs of each moment, and Windhook's resident elemental decided that for this occasion, grandeur was best. From deep within the hull of the House, their elemental made decisions both offensive and defensive. Windhook was never without guidance, even when the family was away.

"Do we know the Flyer?" His question was low, and in the personal House dialect that was nearly indecipherable to those born outside its walls. Vasa shook her head without changing pace as they rounded the primary column to greet the emissary who so desperately wanted them to be frightened.

They were not. They were, however, surprised.

She was young, and imperious, and all of the things that the Crescent Council looked for in new enforcers of their edicts, which were so often catalysts for rebellion that only the finest warriors were even considered for the position. This woman, although a capable flyer, was most certainly not a warrior. In fact, as she stood under the scrutiny of two of the most powerful members of the community, her eyes averted out of habit, for she was a Blightwing—an untouchable, and rarely seen at all near places like House Windhook.

"Welcome, Flyer," Saiinov said, intending to utter nothing further until she observed some degree of decorum. They made be under the eye of the council, but their feet were in House Windhook.

Vasa pasted a neutral smile on her face and followed suit with her silence.

The Blightwing reached into her valise, a beautifully polished piece of young Windbeast, its surface smoothed by countless hands over time. The flap bore the mark of the council: a sphere, then the horizontal, downward crescent, and then a larger sphere beneath; all three shapes were rimmed in black and filled with a blue so vague as to be a rumor. Despite the Flyer's status, she managed a presentable sneer as she lifted the flap and withdrew the faintly luminescent shell on which their request for compliance had been written. The shell was a cylindrical whelk, its ridges perfectly suited for the bold scrawl of a council edict.

Finally, with the shell extended to Vasa, the Blightwing spoke. "You have *one* day cycle, that being today, tonight, and the next day until dusk, in which to respond to this command. Be it known that your crime and complicity is well-documented, and to ignore this evidence is akin to an admission of guilt." She exhaled audibly upon the completion of her scripted accusation.

Vasa's bark of laughter made the messenger visibly flinch, while Saiinov stood with a bemused grin on his face. Neither of the ruling members of House Windhook seemed all that concerned with such a looming threat, sending the Flyer into a measure of alarm at their disregard for her announcement. She began to fidget, and it became clear that her superiors had not prepared her for indifference or outright disdain. The moment lengthened from awkward to sullen, and finally died a merciful death when Saiinov stepped forward and took the shell with measured grace.

"We mean no disrespect to your station or person, Flyer. Please, be welcome here while my wife and I read the demands. You'll rest for the return? Some wine, perhaps?" Saiinov gestured broadly to the wide space of the hall, its colors a cool mesh of blues and gray. The hint of crimson threaded through wall hangings, moving in waves with the pulses of wind. Airy and bright, House Windhook was designed to feel as much a part of the sky as it was a statement of the power that resided within. The Flyer was not unaffected.

"Cressa," she blurted, then flushed under her flyer's tan. Her voice was young and warbled with doubt, now that she spoke on her own behalf.

"Cressa, then." Vasa inclined her head genially, taking a glass of wine from Saiinov and pressing it into the messenger's hand without asking. "From our own bottles. It's light and fortified. Please make yourself comfortable; we won't take long."

"And we will give your message proper consideration. You may be assured this is no bit of theater," Saiinov added as they moved away in syncopation. Decades of marriage let them adopt the same graceful step without thought or planning. Cressa sat down at a carved backless chair, her body somewhere between rigid and desirous of savoring the space around her. As a Blightwing, she had enjoyed few opportunities to do anything for her own pleasure that didn't involve a direct order.

Behind the woven barrier that separated Saiinov's workspace, Vasa began to scan the shell's densely written lines of ink. "It's an opening gambit, of course, but it could be worse. They know about Keiron."

"How could they not? I heard his departure from a distant cloudbank. He didn't go quietly." The scream had been long, and primal. The sound was the cry of a wounded animal fading into the distance. He remained unsettled by the memory, despite knowing that, in part, they had been responsible for its creation.

"Which leads them to our doorstep. They're not charging us with treason for allowing him to go." Vasa's lips pressed into a grim line. She was a mother, and wife, and leader, but she was also free. An incursion into their lives for any reason was most unwelcome, but her expression was nearly toxic with fearful resistance.

"Tell me, dear heart." Saiinov's request was almost delicate with regard for her torment.

When she looked up from the shell there were tears in her eyes, and he knew that something had gone terribly wrong with their plan. "It's not us being called to justice. It's Garrick. They're charging him with murder."

CHAPTER SEVEN:

Tuesday

*a*t precisely nine in the morning, Livvy creaked into her chair and looked around, relieved that she could rest. The walk up had been slow, tedious, and bland, but she made it and could now let her heart catch up with the rest of her. In a moment, she felt stable; in three, she felt bright and prepared. It was Tuesday, which appeared to be a special day at the library. There were balloons festooning a conference room in the distant corner, along with a banner that welcomed a reading club from a school she didn't want to recognize. It was her own, which was blessing and curse, based on her mixed experiences over the past three years.

While she tried to decipher the group's name, Dozer slid into his chair, out of breath and grinning. His eyes were merry with some kind of trouble, so Livvy pretended to look at her pen until he broke the ice.

"You *cannot* act like you don't care about what I have to say." His mock anger accompanied an elevated finger pointing at the conference room. "Are you even aware of the evil about to inhabit that room?"

"Evil? Do we rent to demons?"

"Don't be sassy. That's my job, and to my knowledge, Miss Henatis is the only *actual* demon currently employed within the library's walls. Although the girls down there will come a close second." Dozer leaned back in his chair, forehead lifted in shock that she wasn't at the very least mildly curious about who would be inhabiting the corner conference room.

"Fine," she groused. "Tell me, since you won't let me work until I've made a total fuss over how clever and well-connected you are."

"Those are excellent points that also happen to be true." He leaned forward to deliver the news, his voice dropping to an intimate storyteller's rhythm. "There are only three girls, and they're all perfectly horrible. They alternate between complaining about our cell phone signal in here and when they're going to get free from this prison." He nodded sagely at her in dismissal of such crass behaviors. "You'll get a full dose tomorrow. They were in here once before, but you missed them. I can give you a full report, but only if you go to lunch with me."

"Are you still trying to hustle me into going to the hot dog place on the river? A girl's got to have standards, you know." Livvy looked at her nails with the same bored expression Dozer was using. She was willing to negotiate for a better lunch spot, and wasn't above fighting just a little bit dirty in doing so. If she could be convinced to wander somewhere for a greasy hot dog on a sodden bun, then he could afford to think of something that had a bit more panache.

"You're doing it again." Dozer sniffed at her disregard of his culinary decisions.

"Doing what?"

"You seem to have forgotten — in one day, mind you — that I can more or less read your thoughts. So, with that little tidbit in mind, do you want to reconsider your staunch position on Frankly, Frank's? I mean, I *did* mention that I'm buying, right?" He smiled winningly at her, his eyes crinkled with irrepressible good humor.

Livvy weighed her options. She could of course beg off, given the distance, but Dozer's unspoken belief that she could make it downstairs and back during lunchtime swayed her. Maybe he knew something of her reserves that she didn't. "I accept your offer, but I'd like a clarification."

"Go on." He was the picture of grace, tipping his head to her with great dignity.

"Why are we talking about lunch when we just got here?"

"Ahh, an excellent question, and one that I'm quite willing to answer." He leaned back in his chair and adopted the pose of a lecturer. "Lunch, and more specifically Frankly, Frank's, is the most important meal of the day for you. I could bore you with charts and data and testimonials about how critical this entire event really is, but why not let the product speak for itself?" He spread his hands like a welcoming king, smirking all the while.

"You seem quite confident that your selection is going to be to my liking." Livvy was picky, and no pushover.

"Ahem. Well, yes. *As* your new bestie, I think it's only logical that I would know what I'm doing, right?" He took her hand, and his smile softened. "I wouldn't ask you to go anywhere that you can't, Livvy. I think you'll feel wonderful. There's a lot to be said for a good, clean breath of air in the great outdoors, isn't there?"

"I wouldn't know," she began, and his face was so crestfallen she patted the air in apology. "No, I mean — yes. Take me to lunch, and let's see. Sorry, just not used to *doing*. Because of this thing." She looked at the scar on her chest. "I've always been more of a distant observer. But this is nice. I like having something to look forward to."

"Told ya. You won't even know where the time went." Dozer really could be smug.

But he was right. Three hours flickered by like passing headlights, and Livvy found herself standing, walking with Dozer and, for the first time in her memory, actually *excited* about something over the horizon. They went slowly, with Dozer babbling away, partially because he liked to talk, but also because it took the burden of speech away from her while she concentrated on breathing. In moments, they were outside in the brilliance of spring, and Livyy thought she might cry from the simple pleasure of a friend, and the sun, and their shared sky.

"He's just over there."

And Frank was. His cart was, to put it mildly, a gleaming monstrosity that shined with offensive metallic brilliance.

"He certainly seems to like chrome," she whispered. It seemed polite and took less effort.

Dozer snorted with delight. "Technically, that's stainless steel, but I see what you mean. It is a bit like a spaceship. Or a robot." He made a thoughtful noise before adding, "Maybe both."

Their approach was not unnoticed, despite some minor bustle around the cart. It was a bright day, and the river seemed to sparkle with a vibrancy that let Livvy see into the shallows. She saw shadows moving, and then the odd flash of a silver scale. Fish darted about in their secret world, doing things she could not understand, but that delighted her in the knowing that there was a level beneath her own, filled to bursting with drama and life. A goose honked overhead, then another as they returned from their long sojourn to a place where they would raise their young in a cycle of such antiquity that it would go on well after the last human had drawn a breath. Livvy felt light and free. It was so unusual she had to consider the sensation, but delicately, as if her gaze alone might cause the mood to collapse.

"It is beautiful." Dozer squinted down at her, the light surrounding his face as he smiled with the pleasure of a task undone. "But, we're here to see Frank, not just gawk at the ducks like some goofy tourists." He turned to Frank, a man in neat attire with a hat that sat cocked at a jaunty angle. He was late in life, but hale and beaming with purpose. "I've brought a friend, and I have her convinced that she needs lunch here to make everything better. Livvy is *very* special, so you'd better be on top of your game. What's good today?"

Frank's smile blossomed without reserve at the compliment. "You know the answer to that, Dozer. Can't you read minds?" He gave Livvy a conspiratorial wink and folded his arms, content to watch Dozer sputter with indignation.

"Of course I can, but, well, this *is* your area of expertise. I wouldn't presume to tell an expert how to conduct his business. It's beneath me." His sniff of disdain was nearly inaudible in the river breeze.

Livvy snickered, covering her mouth with a hand before opening it again to laugh with a genuine lack of concern for her heart. It was a rare thing, and Dozer took it in stride as payment rendered to see his friend enjoying herself.

"We'll take two, and let's see where we go from there." Dozer tried to pay, but Frank waved him off with a laugh.

"Not today. Not for this one." Frank bent to his work, and Livvy could see that there was no grease, and no stale buns, or sad onions that looked as if their better days were long past. Everything was fresh, and clean, and as new as the day around them. "For Livvy. Try a bit of that and tell me it isn't a taste of heaven."

Livvy's face was split with limitless joy, until she bit down. "I can't — " She choked, her voice little more than a strangled cough.

"What's wrong?" Dozer lowered his eyes to meet hers, pulling the food away without breaking their gaze. Frank was busy with other customers, his attention elsewhere.

Livvy did not, under any circumstances, want to ruin things by crying, but she did. Tears raced down both cheeks as her skin went pale. "I — something's wrong, I can't."

"You don't have to, honey. It's fine. Let's sit down, want to?" Dozer was moving her without asking, the food already forgotten. They found an angled bench and sat, not speaking. It was some time before her quiet cry ran its course, leaving her bitter and tired. "We don't have to talk about it unless you want to. Back to work, maybe? I can handle the desk, you just sit and be still."

She was too tired and confused to do anything but nod. The whole sad event was a first for her; even at her sickest, she could always eat. Dozer, good as his word, took her on the painstaking walk back to the library, and for the next hour, she couldn't remember anything except the rubbery taste of her failure to enjoy something as wondrous as a meal with a friend.

It was, in fact, just an hour until Livvy felt like her grin was anything other than a complete lie, but she knew the moment it changed. It was 2:59, and she'd just returned from the breakroom. Her lips were moist, her breathing even, and her heart was a gentle patter when he walked through the doors.

There are boys, and there are men. He was neither, caught in that dusk between the two where the beauty of youth isn't overcome by the rugged demands of adulthood. He was tall and narrow at the waist, but broad at the shoulders. He was long, with a lean frame that promised what was to come in the years to follow, his curly black hair slipping forward on his brow like an ebon wave. When his eyes found her, she saw points of light in their black pupils, but it might have been a trick under the glare of the library's erratic bulbs. He smiled, a hesitant thing that was as much a question as a movement.

Livvy smiled back, and felt her hand go to the lock of hair that gave her shelter from the storm of a world filled with nasty surprises for people like her. Sometimes she wore glasses as a further defense, but today she realized they were lost or forgotten. Maybe both, given that she didn't quite seem herself.

"Annnnnd . . . contact." Dozer was smirking as he muttered to her. Leave it to him; he'd seen their recognition of each other the instant it occurred. He really was quite observant, although his smugness was irksome.

"Hush, you." There was no time for anything else, so Livvy looked up, pasted a wary smile on her face, and regarded the stranger as he stood looking down at her with a smile of relief.

"Please tell me — information desk?" He waved a hand at the lack of signage, but his smile never faded.

In her life, Livvy had been on four dates. One was a neighbor, who had been shoved into her driveway by an exuberant relative as if he was doing the world a great favor by paying attention to her. Granted, she'd been at that *truly* horrible age of a newly minted fifteen year old, where her legs were long, her hair was frizzy, and her fashion choices ranged from bad to worse. Still, Livvy wasn't going to be anyone's anthropology project, so she sent him on his way after two sips of warm soda and a conversation that was nearly as flat.

Her second and third dates had been, if it was possible, even worse. They were both with the same guy, a reasonably normal upperclassman who had been friendly to Livvy for two years. The first date was a movie in which she sat so still that her butt began to sweat; a fact that mortified her beyond belief, since she was certain the skin of her legs would come off on the plastic chair bottom. The fact they hadn't even held hands sent her into a long night of self-examination and worry. Exhausted and frayed, she was utterly stunned when he called the next day and asked her to go to an actual restaurant for actual food. Her mother had begun a whirlwind process of grooming and dressing her that rivalled most royal weddings, leaving Livvy slightly tired but looking more like a woman than she'd ever dreamed. To her relief, her dad opted to spend the entire day in the yard hunting crabgrass and dandelions, but mostly he was intentionally absent from the torrent of activity that it took to get Livvy ready for a date.

Todd picked her up on time. He was polite and attentive, and when they were done eating, he casually informed her that he was joining the Navy and wanted nothing more than to have someone's picture to show his classmates in the Great Lakes Naval Station.

"I always thought you were sorta hot, even though you can't really do nothin', but I gotta leave in six days and I figured we could hook up before. You're not seeing nobody, right?" Todd had asked in such a matter-of-fact way that Livvy sat stunned, looking at the remains of cold lasagna on her plate.

It made her vaguely sick. She hadn't been able to touch the dish since, but she managed not to cry or so much as utter a sound until Todd dropped her off without pulling in her driveway. Livvy closed the car door with a pointed click and never looked back, until just this year when a barista asked her out as she was ordering a caffeine-free caramel frappe that looked more like a milkshake than a coffee drink. She'd nearly choked, but after some thought she said yes. He was handsome in the way that intellectuals can be, with floppy hair and an air of indolence, even when he was working.

He showed up at her house, patiently listened to Livvy's mom explain that she was not to be out past eleven, and said, "Yeah, I kinda don't do the whole curfew thing. Thanks, but nah. You were in over your head anyway." He'd pulled away to leave Livvy standing on her sidewalk, wondering if having half a heart meant that she was half a person, and only entitled to half of everything, including love and respect.

And now, here she was again, looking up at someone whose eyes were fixed on her so intently he seemed to be part cat, which would have been weird if she didn't like cats.

He smiled again before repeating, "Is this the information desk?" His tone was light but not teasing.

"We are. I mean, it is. They are, too," Livvy sputtered, but Dozer intervened as smoothly as an attorney summing up a case. His gallantry was on tap at all times, especially during social crises of the current magnitude.

"This is the information desk, and Livvy here will be happy to assist you. And you are?" Dozer's brow rose with a paternal shift, before settling into something friendlier. He was slipping into the role of her enforcer like it was a favorite pair of shoes.

"Keiron. And I think I'm in the right place, Livvy." He held out a hand.

She took it. His skin was warm and dry, and the pressure between the hands was exactly right; he had nothing to prove except the certainty of his touch. It was a connection in the open, and all the more enticing because of that fact. They both smiled, and Dozer sighed like a matron watching her last daughter be asked to dance at a ball.

"I need a terminal to use. Can you sign me on?" He looked over his shoulder at the bank of cubbies with private computers and screens. The regulars had a few tied up, but there were several open.

"Sure, let me get you a guest pass." She printed a small slip of paper with the access code for visitors. "You've got two hours, but if you need more and we're not busy, you can just come get another one. We're not really supposed to, but it'll be fine." Livvy's smile was both shy and admiring.

Keiron took the paper and let his eyes flicker down to the massive scar that ran up her chest. He looked, he saw, he moved on, no judgement or notice in his features whatsoever.

"Great, thanks. I can do this every day?" He looked mildly surprised, as if he'd been expecting some kind of problem.

"Sure, just not on Sunday. We're closed." She regretted the existence of Sunday at all, if he would be visiting each day.

"Not Sunday. Okay. I'll have my project wrapped up by then, promise." He gave her a jaunty salute and wandered past the table to an open terminal, but not before saying, "If you get bored, come help. I'm lousy with technology."

Her only answer was a stunned nod, but she shook her head lightly as the moment faded from embarrassment to curiosity. Livvy wasn't scared. She was interested, and for the first time in her life, she'd been recognized. The sensation agreed with her.

Lup lup lup. Her heart went a bit faster, but she paid it no mind. If Keiron could ignore it, then for at least a moment, so could she.

CHAPTER EIGHT:

Flyer

*I*t was a long, silent wait before Saiinov and Vasa emerged into the main hall. They did so in the fugue state of parents who had gotten bad news that couldn't be ignored, but must be digested slowly, so that their minds would not spin off howling into the night. Adults are built, not born, and good parents can armor themselves against anything under the sun in order to protect their family.

But they have a weakness.

Their children are both their cause and their downfall. Children *need* their families, but the greatest secret never told is that at some point, this ceases to be true. The opposite, however, is not. Parents will ease into life watching their children grow and struggle, and win and lose, but there is always a terrible moment when it becomes apparent that the dynamic has changed.

Children grow up, and they stop needing their parents, unless something drastic, unholy, and swift happens to them.

Like an accusation of murder.

Saiinov and Vasa walked slowly to Cressa, who sat in her odd pose, eyes darting about the great space with the discomfort of a Blightwing who had entered a place that was not her own. She was a plain girl, young and tidy, with a long nose and the dark eyes of an easterner. Her black hair was pulled back to reveal a long neck and square shoulders. Cressa's mouth was small but mobile, and when not concentrating, she had the unlined face of a newborn. She certainly didn't *look* like a murderer, but the pattern of her wings fading from gray to black declared for all the world that she had unjustly taken another life.

"Cressa." Saiinov's voice was leaden as he addressed her, all formality gone. "We apologize for any undue delay. This is a bit of a shock."

Vasa's wintry smile told the messenger it was most certainly more than a shock; it was, in fact, a declaration of war by the council. What House Windhook would do in response could change the course of time. Cressa knew this, so she nodded respectfully and waited for them to conclude their thoughts.

Vasa pointed to a portrait hanging nearby. A boy of no more than ten held a tiny Windbeast, its wriggling coils around one forearm as he laughed and stroked the creature's gangly body. His flying boots were wet from play, and one sleeve of his tunic had a tear in it, untended and forgotten. He didn't look anything like the people before her; where they were regal, he was playful, even joyous. Vasa watched the messenger take in details from the portrait, then she walked to it and traced the line of Keiron's jaw. It was still soft, like a baby's, although there was something underneath that spoke to the possibility of a man. But not yet.

"Keiron was not born within the more common schools of power, but we knew that when we first looked upon him. He's a beautiful boy. He was *always* a beautiful boy, but so kind and soft. He is rounded in a world that would rather he were all dangerous edges." Vasa's words were nearly lost in the room, so soft had she spoken. "When he opened his eyes, I knew that he was not truly mine. Oh, to be sure, I carried him, and felt his hard little feet and hands drumming about—do you remember when he knocked the glass off my belly, how we laughed?" Her eyes cut to Saiinov, who smiled sadly in remembrance. "He was the last of six children, all of them driven, sculpted. Perfect."

Tears began to fall, and Cressa felt a shame so intense she had to look away. This was too private for her to witness. It didn't feel like the love of a parent. The moment was more like the burial of a family.

"Lady, I—" Cressa began, but faltered. What was she to say? I apologize for bringing you news that your second favorite son is to be seized and trussed up like I was? That he will be spat upon, and stripped, and then hurled to a death so ghastly that no record will be kept, for fratricide is a crime so black that not even the council will keep record of it? Instead, she said, "They are not coming for Keiron. He is dead, I am told. They come for Garrick, who is not only alive, but nearby. Although in truth, no one with the council knows where he is. They think he ran away after the incident."

"Incident?" Vasa's question was a single word of pure frost. After her emotions cooled, she affixed Cressa with a patient gaze. "Do you know who I am?" There was no arrogance in her question.

Cressa could sense that a lesson waited in the answer, so she merely shook her head.

"My husband is a Skywatcher, but I am the Scholar. It is I who dives into the lore, and the records, and the half-remembered lies of a time so distant that there were no Houses, only flocks of errant souls darting to and fro with no purpose. No science. No writing. Imagine a time like that, can you?"

"I cannot." And Cressa couldn't, although she thought that a world without the council would be a fine thing indeed.

Vasa locked her hands behind her and began to pace, occasionally stabbing the air with the authority of a born teacher. "Garrick did not kill his brother, because it isn't possible."

"It's not?" Cressa was genuinely surprised. She'd seen numerous denials of crime, but nothing so outrageous as a parent saying their child was immortal. Nothing was immortal, not even the stars.

Vasa's smile was conspiratorial. She stole a glance at Saiinov, who wore an inscrutable mask. "Keiron isn't Windborn," she began, and there was pride in her words at the repeated declaration of her child's unusual status.

That made Cressa furrow her brow in open revolt at the idea of anyone not wanting to be Windborn. Their kind ruled the greatest of houses, and sorcery, and power in general. To be Windborn was — - she hesitated, thinking it was the opposite of everything she felt. Rare, and feared, but respected. They were valued beyond belief in their society that prized status and ability above talent alone; to be of their school at birth meant that nothing was beyond their reach. The Windborn produced heroes of all kinds, and names that were spoken in hushed tones.

Vasa saw this and raised a hand in supplication. "I understand; to say such a thing is unthinkable. Who wouldn't want to be a part of the elite, sending child after child into the ranks of Scholars, and Skywatchers, and even the secretive Watershapers and their legendary arcana?"

"I meant no disrespect, Lady." Cressa realized her error in judgement, but Vasa only smiled gently at the imaginary offense.

"You did not offend us, Flyer. You confirmed the very reasons why we celebrate Keiron's birth as one of the Heartborn." Saiinov inclined his head politely as he began to explain something that might seem like sheer mutiny to a Blightwing. "Have you, before today, heard of House Windhook?" He didn't look at Cressa as he spoke. His attention was on a distant bank of nimbus clouds. A large, bulbous shape moved within, before diving deeper into the secret folds of the storm that brewed to the south. His eyes followed the creature until it faded into obscurity. *Good hunting to you*, Saiinov thought as the predator's passing was little more than a swirl in the clouds.

"Yes. I — of course. You're the most powerful House outside the Crescent Council. Your vote and favor can sway an issue because you are beholden to no one thing or cause." Cressa grinned apologetically, adding, "And they hate you for it, even as they crave your guidance and your support."

Saiinov and Vasa laughed together, but gently. There was an element of humor in being both loved and hated, yet it was a mantel they wore easily. If anything, their staunch refusal to join the council had kept them free. House Windhook used that status to grow in power and prestige, even while others brawled in political chambers for position in a hierarchy that was designed for constant uproar. Looking out over the peaceful skies, Cressa could see the logic in their position.

Cressa stood as if to leave, but the waver in her step meant that there were things unsaid. In the current situation, that was ill advised.

"You have questions, Cressa? We will answer." Vasa's words were firm, polite, and a clear invitation to stay.

Nerves got the best of her, but only for a moment. After watching cloud shadow pass across the floor, she spoke. Cressa's voice was low, even urgent. "How could you let him go?"

Her words hung between the three of them like a foul odor. Perhaps it was too bold, too cutting of her to ask such a thing, but Cressa had little more to give than the truth. As a Blightwing, very little of her life was her own — if any at all. To her relief, it was Vasa who chose to answer. While both she and Saiinov were intimidating, there was something more accessible about Vasa, verging into the realm of kindness. Anyone could see she was a mother, and perhaps that was the thread Cressa detected in the radiant features of the Lady of House Windhook.

"I once heard a council member speaking of her children. This was when I was . . . very young." Vasa smiled at her husband, and there were untold stories in the simple gesture.

Cressa found herself wondering how long they'd been married; it had to be a century or more, given their status as a House.

"I was passing through the secondary halls where the council takes refreshment after hours of pretending to work. As a youth, I was more or less invisible to them, since I had nothing to offer, no leverage or favors to grant. They were a bitter, ancient group even then, but at least three members had living children with which to temper their emotions. Cressa, you may learn someday, children are more than a smaller version of yourself to be doted on and treated like an exotic pet who gets more wild and beautiful with each passing year. No, our children are a glimpse at what our aspirations and love and work may become, but only if we do not relent in our efforts to deliver them a world better than our own. So, when I listened to a council member speak of her own children, I never forgot the mix of pride and bewilderment in her voice. What she spoke of was inconsequential, do you understand? It was the mere fact that all these years later, I can recall her meaning as clearly as if she were standing here now in her resplendent robes, telling a minor tale of a child doing something that meant nothing to anyone but a handful of people. And yet, in the telling of her story, I understood what I was hearing. It was wonder, as if she spoke of a meeting between the gods of air and sky." Vasa paused to collect herself as memories of her own children began to intrude. Her eyes were bright and moist. "Keiron is my son. I carried him, feeling him from the first secretive flutter to the cries of a robust, squalling babe. He was born with his eyes open, did you know that?"

Cressa looked shocked. How could she know such a thing? "No, lady. I, ah, was not present at that event," she replied with great diplomacy in case Vasa had been overcome with grief in the telling of a story that recalled a child now lost.

Vasa's laugh was a warm ripple. "Oh, dear, I do

apologize. No, of course you weren't. I meant that his eyes were open *because* he was Heartborn."

"That is a trait? Of their kind?" Cressa was curious. She knew precious little of the Heartborn; they were not only rare, but left only shadows and whispers behind in the way of lore. Much of their story was rumor and family legend, often inflated to make their house of origin into something more noble than lucky. For that matter, she knew little of infants, save that they tended to cause enormous fuss, like a tiny storm that never really went away.

Saiinov sat down, relaxing somewhat. After their initial tensions, it appeared that he was choosing diplomacy and kindness in the face of Cressa's message. When his face was in repose, it became more handsome than fierce, a fact that she enjoyed as he was close enough that she could see each individual scale in his woven armor. It fluttered over his skin as he breathed, refracting the light from outside in supple waves. He crossed his legs, then dropped his chin into a palm as he regarded the young woman with eyes that were marbled with interest.

"How old are you, Cressa? Please answer only if the question itself gives no offense," Saiinov added. His voice was deep, measured. He even seemed considerate, given the circumstances. They were, after all, discussing the possible seizure and end to House Windhook.

"Seventeen, sir." She waited, unsure what to do next. While she was permitted to leave, it seemed bad form, given their decision to treat her with the respect due her station, despite her status as a Blightwing. She found herself looking down at the storm-gray feathers that curled around her, cursing each vane of every one for branding her as a monster. She didn't feel like a monster, but her wings said differently in a society obsessed with status and power.

Saiinov smiled, and it was a warm, living thing that made Cressa regret her purpose even more. "Dear heart, do you even remember *being* seventeen?"

Vasa glared playfully at him. "I do, and you would be well served to never ask such a question again. I'm told that there are any number of unoccupied territories to the west where a comedian of your caliber would enjoy spending some time alone with his thoughts."

He patted the air in surrender before clearing his throat. "Ahh, but of course. Before my crass outburst, I was asking your age. It wasn't an entirely idle question, Cressa." He grew serious, pointing to her wings. "You're young, and faced with an uncertain future at best, and exile or death at worst. Please believe me when I say I am sorry for that fact."

"As am I," Vasa chimed in. She meant it.

"I sense that there is something else you'd like to discuss besides my status as a pariah, sir." Cressa gave them both a neutral look, then waited. She learned quickly how to force the issue in a conversation. She was young, but clever.

Vasa asked with some urgency, "Have you ever met a Heartborn before?"

Cressa thought hard before reaching her conclusion. "Once, if you could even call it a meeting. I was very young."

"Where was this? Can you remember?" Saiinov looked interested by her admission, no matter how vague.

"I was very small. My family was at a gathering of houses in the Eastern Reaches." She smiled apologetically while sifting memories for detail. "It was a busy place. I mostly remember colors and sounds, not the purpose of why we were there. My oldest sister was carrying me on her hip. I *do* know that, because Meri was always so kind to me, even when I would pull at her wings and hair. I suspect I was quite a little beast, but she had nothing but patience for me."

"Sisters will do that." Vasa looked pleased to know that bit of history.

Even Saiinov allowed her a gentle laugh. They clearly knew children.

"It got loud. There was a dispute over something, and when I asked Meri, she would only say that it was *grownup business*, meaning that we would ignore it and go look for sweets. I was playing with her strand of windpearls as we made our way through the crowd to the vendors who cried out from the edges of the fray. There were many, many faces, but I only remember the one."

"The Heartborn?" Vasa asked.

Cressa nodded, her lips pursed as she sought the words to explain a chance encounter from years earlier. "He was an island of quiet in all the tumult. I remember that he walked by us, and people were pointing, only to fall silent in the wake of his passage. I don't think he was much older than I am right now, but people deferred to him without hesitation. I've met Windborn, and Cloudborn, and I think I might have been near a family made of entirely of Lightborn. My skin felt alive just being in the room with that bunch." She made a face. Lightborn were notoriously prone to out-bursts of passion and erratic behavior, but there was no doubt as to the strength in their houses. The Windborn and Cloudborn were both immensely powerful, but more stable and likely to utilize sober reflection and study rather than brute excitement to achieve their goals. All of the most lethal abilities were sprinkled across the skies where people lived and built their Houses into towering reservoirs of strength and influence.

All save one. The Heartborn.

Their numbers were incredibly rare, and moreover, the reason was unknown. It was suspected that because of their great gifts, it was a natural means of balancing the distribution of power between the people, as even two Heartborn in one House might be seen as virtually unstoppable in all pursuits. Rumors of entire familial lines of Heartborn in the North were just that — rumors.

Vasa and Saiinov shared a look as they prepared to ask Cressa more about meeting someone like their son. Keiron inspired the same kind of reactions with everyone except Garrick. "Do you remember anything of the event? Why a Heartborn would be there?" Vasa's question was spoken low, as if they neared a truth that would be uncomfortable to speak aloud.

"There were council guards, and they were armed. The sun on their crests and weapons was nearly blinding, and they seized a man who was standing on a column, shouting at the crowd. Before they could take him away, the Heartborn stepped forward and pushed their spears down with his finger. He wasn't scared; I remember that. I think he was smiling, as if he was meant to be there in the midst of all that anger." Cressa looked ashamed, as if she was somehow responsible for what was to come. "My sister told me to look away, and I heard — something. It was a terrible noise, like the keening of a Skyhawk as it dives to save one of its young. When I opened my eyes, the crowd was dispersing, and the man who had been in custody was standing by himself. No one would look at him or approach him." Her face burned with high spots of color before she whispered, "The way people treat me now."

Saiinov poured something cold into a fluted glass and held it to Cressa, waiting patiently until her hand was steady enough to take it. She sipped gratefully, collecting herself with each passing second. Being a Blightwing was something she couldn't escape, but occasionally there were reminders that made it far worse. Like now.

"Was the Heartborn still there, after the people began to leave?" Vasa watched Cressa's color return to something more normal. The fortifying drink was helping, as was their regard for her as a person and not some foul thing.

"No." One word, little more than a whisper. Cressa looked down into the unseen depths below, seeking to hide from the memory.

Saiinov and Vasa rose as one to kneel before her. Both of their faces were soft with understanding, but something painful lurked there as well. Cressa reminded herself that she was here to take, not understand, and it made the next moments even more difficult.

Vasa took her hand in the manner of one who has calmed her children with a deft touch. "Dear Flyer, ask me again how it is that we could let him go." Her voice was soft, encouraging.

Cressa wove between silence and the need to know before blurting, "How?"

Vasa unleashed the terrible truth with a smile of such resigned sadness that Cressa nearly looked away. "Because he was never really ours to begin with."

CHAPTER NINE:

Wednesday

*L*ivvy normally had an excellent memory, but she couldn't recall a thing from her wait to see if Keiron would in fact be at the library every day. It was Wednesday, which was different than Tuesday, so when he walked through the doors at 10:02, Livvy's breath caught in a noise between relief and joy.

"He's just a boy, Liv." Dozer was pretending to work, but his knowing look said otherwise.

She didn't look away, but cast an arch glance sideways before resuming her observation. "He's not *just* anything, you cretin."

At Dozer's snort of laughter, she turned to see him wallowing in smugness. "You've known him for a day and I can troll you with five words." His voice dropped into a lower register, and he took on a serious look while pointing at her with a pen. "Doctor Dozer has examined you, and the news isn't good, young lady. I'm afraid this case of *Library Crush* is fatal." He pretended to scrawl something on scrap paper and handed it to her with a flourish. "Take a ten minute stroll with Keiron and call me after lunch."

Keiron arrived at the desk and politely ignored their banter; he'd have to be truly tone deaf not to notice that their byplay was most likely about him. Livvy's face was delightfully flushed, and Dozer wore an expression of such smugness that he looked feline.

"Hey, Livvy. Like I said, every day until I'm done." He waved expansively at the shelves and desks, an irrepressible grin on his lips. His hair was windblown, the curls in a riot against order. Livvy fought the urge to pat them in place, wondering where such boldness was coming from.

"I for one am glad you are here." She froze with mortification at her selection of words. Apparently, she'd been possessed by the spirit of a British receptionist.

Keiron seized the moment, bowing with an affectation of gallantry. "I too am pleased to be here."

Dozer feigned being busy, a state that he achieved almost instantaneously despite, to Livvy's estimation, not ever doing a single thing that could be construed as actual work. Livvy grimaced before a sunny smile broke out, and she laughed at her own ineptitude. "Words. Ugh. Do you need a computer?"

"I do, but I need to look at reference material, too. I'll probably need a quiet room. I'm not sure I can concentrate unless it's totally silent. Force of habit, I guess." He looked around. The study rooms were either filled with people or dark. "Anything open?"

Dozer pointed helpfully to a single room left of the printer. "That one's still free. Want it?"

"Sure, save it for me? I'm going to look around for a bit. Will you be here?" Keiron looked hopefully at Livvy, who pointed at her desk and nodded.

"Not going anywhere except the break room, and maybe lunch. You've got a while to wander." She smiled as her confidence returned. It was hard *not* to be assured with Keiron smiling at her.

"Good with me. I'll be back." He ambled off somewhere between a walk and a mosey, and Livvy exhaled.

"Correct me if I'm wrong—it's a rare thing, by the way—but I don't think he's back here for research." Dozer's grin was conspiratorial.

Livvy pulled at the lock of hair she used for a talisman, trying hard not to lose her breath over something as simple as a boy. She succeeded, but only just.

"Okay, first things first. That"—Dozer pointed at the errant curl she dragged over one eye—"Doesn't work for me. So no more hiding behind your armor, even if it is an amazing natural color." He grinned and pushed her hair back in a swift, decisive gesture. After a moment in which she felt like a criminal in a lineup, he relented and pushed his chair back slightly. "You shouldn't hide from the world, Liv. It isn't what you were meant to do, no matter how much better you feel covering your face."

She didn't know what to say. For all her life, Livvy had fought to be normal, but really, she'd wanted to be invisible. She was so tired of being tired, and everything that went along with having the cruelest joke of nature rattling along in her chest like an engine that was always at the edge of failure. "I know, but—"

"But what? I'm not trying to say you haven't done an amazing job being you, kid. You have. I just wish you could see what *I* see, that's all." He slid the chair back and took her hand. His touch was warm and assured.

For the first time, Dozer could see the pain she carried with her as the tears began to fall. He pulled a massive stack of tissues out and foisted them on her even as she waved him off, but he took his duties as her self-appointed guardian seriously. She accepted the tissues and promptly blew her nose in a noise that rivaled the geese flying above the river nearby.

"Sorry." She faltered on the edge of control, but lost it again, and this time it looked like it was going to stay.

"What is it, Livvy? What's hurting you right this second? You can tell me." Dozer's request was so soft only she could have heard it. His eyes filled with pain even as she twisted the tissues into a tortured knot before looking up at him. There was panic, then sadness, and finally, something like exhaustion.

"Do you know how many doctors have poked me like an experiment? I can't even remember them all. Sometimes they bring their students in — all of these interested, bland faces, looking at me like I'm just this piece of girl meat that they can't explain. They talk about me like I'm not even in the room, and they swear to my mom and dad that they only what what's best for me, but can't I just stay overnight for some tests and a few more x-rays? They *ooo* and *ahhh* over me, and sometimes, when they think I'm not looking, they actually look happy. My — my heart, or what I have, makes them happy. I don't think they ever *want* to fix me, because then they wouldn't have their toy to play with." She laughed, a short, bitter sound that was far older than she looked. "I'm the best thing that ever happened for them, and when I try to tell them how sad it makes me, I run out of breath and wonder if I'm going to pass out because I cried too hard." She entered a state where her sobs were internal, brutal things, held down by the force of will that a girl had learned to save herself from the curious and the cruel.

Dozer watched her carefully, with the eyes of someone who made his mind up that he was going all in on protecting someone he barely knew. "Well, they'll have to get through me first, Liv." He was so glib, so sold on his own ability, her spirits lifted like they'd been caught in a fresh breeze.

She wiped at her eyes, reflexively putting one hand over her heart like she always did when the darkness and pain were a bit too much at once. "Yeah? Starting when, tough guy?"

Looking past her, his face clouded with moderate disgust as he rolled his eyes. "Like right now." His face split in a horrible, fake smile that made him look like a mannequin with perfect teeth. "Welcome to the second floor. The room you're looking for is just that way, past the third aisle."

Three girls wearing identical outfits stopped just short of the desk. All of them were in a state of permanent huff that left no doubts as to their perceived social positions. Two of them were looking down at their phones, bored, but the third bore the attitude of a ruthless queen. She pointed at Livvy with her phone, gasping in pleased surprise.

"Oh. My. Gawd. It's Wheezer!" A vicious smile lit her face as she leaned on the counter to the left of Dozer as if by sheer closeness the insult would hurt Livvy even more. She was a beautiful girl, with cocoa skin and lurid green eyes that sparkled with ugly joy at seeing Livvy sitting behind the desk, hands folded and a look of mild bewilderment at her outburst. Her friends were oddly symmetrical, both being pretty, dyed blondes with overdrawn eyebrows and makeup that looked like they'd all been watching the same contouring videos on Youtube. "Brit, Ash, look. It's the rare Wheezer, out in the wild."

Livvy smiled, but didn't look away. "Hi, Jessica. I wish I'd known it was you reserving the study room. I would have put coloring books and crayons in it for you."

Dozer snickered, a noise of such wicked delight that the two silent friends of Jessica abandoned their phones and looked up.

They all cocked their heads like curious birds, regarding Livvy and Dozer like a zoo exhibit.

"I take it you know these three runaway models?" he asked Livvy, then gave Jessica a wintry smile of his own before he slid closer to Livvy in an unconscious gesture of solidarity.

Jessica missed the barb, but knew the tone. "As much as I'd love to stand here and chat with the hired help, I'm not going to do that. Which way to our study room?" She plucked at one sleeve to straighten it. In truth, the three of them looked like they could use a quiet place to sit and get themselves together. It was a windy day, and they all showed signs of a long walk outside, or maybe a wrestling match gone wrong. She pulled a cardigan from her bag and tied it around her waist. Britney and Ashley did the same, and soon they all had red sweaters hanging from their narrow hips like triplets who had dressed in the dark.

Dozer pointed, never losing his plastic smile. "Ladies, your room is just down there. It's the one without a light on, sort of like your heads."

Ashley twitched at that, her blue eyes firing with

anger. "I didn't come to this social morgue to be insulted by some bitch with a plastic name tag."

Jessica raised her other brow, before savoring an evil grin of her own. Britney looked confused and started pulling at her lip, which was slightly puffy. She was clearly third of the trio, and had a nervous tic to go with it, but she caught on quickly enough and began muttering under her breath about Livvy. Her brown eyes were flat with anger.

"I cannot *even* with this busted pair," Jessica finally muttered, which seemed to be the official close to the meet-and-greet. She waved her phone as the three turned without a word and began leaving like a school of fish, their steps taking them haltingly down the aisles to the one dark room.

Livvy watched the light flick on as they began to negotiate seats, all with a uniformly bland look of disinterest on their faces. They had book bags but no laptops, and it looked like they were in for a dull stay.

"Thanks. I sort of hate them." Livvy pulled her attention back to Dozer, who looked at the three girls thoughtfully.

"You'd think that girls like that would know better, but they don't."

"Know what?" Livvy fidgeted with a pen as she waited for his full attention.

"They called you Wheezer, and they're all so wrapped up in their own drama that they can't even look you in the eye. It's going to cost them someday." He sighed, and it was an old, tired sound. "Acting like an ass comes to them as easily as breathing. I wonder if they'll always be like that, or if something will bring it crashing down." It was a moment of remarkable depth for Dozer, who had up until then seemed content to take the world around him as it came, albeit with a good dose of snark.

"They've been that way since we started school together. I mostly stayed out of their way, but two years ago something happened that put me on their radar. It's been bad ever since then," she admitted.

"What did you do? Steal the prom title?" Dozer's tone said that he thought Livvy could pull it off.

Her cheeks rose with color at his opinion of her beauty, especially because he was being purely honest. She liked it. She shook her head, grinning. "Even worse. Stole their thunder. A local news channel found out about me and sent a reporter to school. He was going to do a sort of human interest thing. I hated the idea, but mom and dad thought it might help me, umm. Well, they thought it might help, that's all." She began closing up emotionally, but Dozer was having none of it.

"Help with what? And don't play dumb. You're not." He leaned back in his chair, the picture of indolence. He could wait.

"A heart transplant. You know, get my story back out there again. It was — people knew me, but the story just came and went, you know? Sometimes we would get emails from people who said they were adding my name to another database, but other times it was just quiet. Too quiet, my mom would say. She always wanted there to be some new interest, or source, or whatever just to make sure that people didn't forget I was different." She fought mightily to contain her maudlin side. Livvy was sick, not sappy, which was good because Dozer wouldn't tolerate self-pity.

He considered that for some time before *tsking* like an

old aunt. "I knew they were shallow, but that seems excessive even for people like them. I guess there's no limit to what girls will do to each other." He smiled ruefully before brightening. "Shouldn't you go find Keiron and give him the tour? Or at least pretend to?" Dozer's face gleamed with conspiracy. It was easy to see that he had ulterior motives for Lizzy, and those plans could not be enacted from behind a desk.

"I guess . . ." She drew out the word, but still managed to stand up without seeming too eager.

Dozer waved her away in a shooing motion, his face beaming. She took a few steps, waited, and then went on past the first tables. Keiron was nowhere to be seen, but Danny caught her eye. He looked pleased to see her, even ceasing the tapping of his fingers long enough to wave.

"Hey, Livvy. Out for a stroll with the animals, eh?" His lopsided grin made him seem even more like a hippie who got lost in a library.

Miss Willie made a sound of reproach but didn't look up from her book. They were sitting together at a table that was organized with nearly maniacal perfection. Everything on it was at a right angle, even the book that Miss Willie was reading.

"I like being a zookeeper. Especially when you critters love reading. What've you got?" She looked down at the thick tome open in front of him.

"*The Science of Sleep*," he said with something like a flourish. "It's wonderful. A bit heavy for the layman, but worth my time. There's a lot to be said for understanding the human mind and body."

"Makes me tired just looking at it," Miss Willie chimed in. She clearly didn't share Danny's enthusiasm for the topic.

Livvy laughed at their camaraderie. "I'm with Miss Willie. Why not read something, I don't know —"

"Less nerdy?" Danny asked, his face split with a coy grin. "Can't help it. A man needs to know certain things, and this" — he hefted the book — "is one of them."

Livvy bowed her head slightly at his dedication. "I'll leave you to it then." She smiled and stepped away, even as Danny began to mumble, reading words to himself in a low drone.

Miss Willie didn't seem to notice. *Point in her favor*, thought Livvy, and before she could finish her rumination, Keiron was there.

He was even taller than when they'd met at the desk, and she couldn't figure out why. "I like it," she said into the silence between them.

He stopped short and looked at her with a furtive half-smile that fit his face perfectly.

"Did I say that out loud?"

"You did, so now I have to ask what exactly it is that you like. If it's ice cream, or giraffes, or even hot air balloons, then there is absolutely every reason to affirm that you like those things for no reason. But if it's something weird, like your fascination with amateur yodeling, then we might have to slow down on our friendship. A guy's gotta have standards, you know." He took a step forward, his smile never fading.

It was her turn to be cute, but all she could think of was, "Is there such a thing as professional yodeling? I mean, how would you get paid? And, umm . . . what do people yodel for? Is it a call, like there's some animal named the yodel that responds to the cry of highly trained people?"

Her lips curled even as she tried to remain stern. It wasn't working, not really. He was too close, and his interest seemed too real.

Keiron leaned against the nearest bookshelf and adopted a teaching persona. "To the untrained ear, mountain calls are all alike. But here, at the finest yodeling school in the history of the universe, you will learn to hone your voice into a well-oiled machine, capable of summoning even the most distant—" He stopped, puzzled. "Huh. I don't know why they do it either. I just know they always seem to be in mountains, and dressed in some kind of leather shorts that look kind of like battle armor. Seems rather uncomfortable to me."

"I'll pass," Livvy said with shake of her head. "Mountains? Too tall. Leather shorts? Too much chafing."

"You don't like mountains?" He seemed surprised. There were hills nearby, but they weren't actually mountains. More like really aggressively heaped mounds of dirt.

"Nope. Can't breathe that high up." She laughed, then covered her scar reflexively. "I can't even really breathe down here, for that matter."

"What about down here? You mean the library?" His eyes were soft and dark above a generous mouth, with lips that curled when he seemed to hold back a laugh, which was often. Keiron was far from dour.

Livvy looked around before answering. It was a trick she acquired to give herself time to breathe, but just then it was more out of habit. "I guess I mean everywhere. I can't run, not that I ever would—who wants to run? I mean, just take off and run? Unless there's a bear after me, it's not happening."

Keiron ticked off points on his fingers. "Okay, so no running. And I'm just guessing, but no bears either? I've never actually met one, but I'm told that they can be moody." When she nodded, he went on. "No leather shorts, but that just makes sense. I wouldn't wear wooden shorts either, and those are kind of the same thing."

"Right. So, we're back to the original point. I have a hard time breathing, but I kinda want to show you the library because I really do like it here." She spread her hands to indicate their current impasse, which wasn't really anything of the sort. It was just a lull in their conversation.

Keiron held up a finger. "A solution, if I may?"

"Go on," she allowed, hoping his idea was a good one. It was.

"I propose that you walk in whichever direction you'd like. I'll follow. You can show me the whole library and tell me why you like it, and then when we're done I'll act like we weren't flirting, and you can pretend I really do care about the multimedia room and how many water fountains you have. Sound good?"

She blushed but held out an arm. Livvy could do this. She knew it. "I accept your kind offer. Do you have any further conditions?" If this was flirting, then Livvy couldn't imagine what it felt like to fly.

"I do." His voice was grave, even dignified.

She waited, but he said nothing until she poked him, looking up with a grin that told him he needed to speak now or forever hold his peace.

"Just one thing," Keiron began. He looked down at her like she was a deer ready to bolt, knowing that the next words he spoke needed to be perfect. They were. "We'll take it slow," he said, leaving the meaning to her.

So they did.

An hour later, Livvy sat in the break room, wrapped in a mix of excitement and curiosity. She sipped at her water, but didn't really notice how flat and warm it was. She didn't really notice anything just then, because she was too busy turning over her time with Keiron, flipping it in her mind to look from every angle.

From any direction, her walk with him looked good. He was kind, and a bit goofy, and smart. He seemed to know a little about everything as they wove their way through the aisles of books who stood in mute observation of their dance. She learned that he was a youngest child, and he loved his parents, but only liked four of his siblings. He thought it was better to be kind and bold, but it got him into trouble that he didn't regret. Keiron disliked swimming but loved the ocean waves, and he'd never seen a living fish. He respected his father but feared him a little, and he loved his mother more than anything in the heavens because of all his family, only she knew to let him be when he was quiet. Keiron was far from perfect, and if she was being honest, their lives seemed to be similar in strange and wondrous ways.

She let him speak, listening to the beautiful boy's story come to life through his words like a painting that suddenly began to move, revealing centuries of flaws that added to the mystery and story. Livvy decided right there that she liked the details.

He had cracks, and those were what made him good.

When they reached an alcove that was filled with two low shelves of books, he set his feet and leaned back, looking out the bay window. The river ran silently below, people moving alongside on their way to places unknown, but somewhere different from where they stood under the modest sunshine. Clouds were building in the west, a low band of gray that began to nip hungrily at the bright blue sky.

For the first time in their hour together Keiron took on an air of authority, but it was a gentle kind. "Enough about my petty squabbles with Garrick." He waved a hand around the library. "Why here? What makes you come here? Are books your refuge?" His smile crinkled at the corners of his eyes.

Livvy felt dangerously light inside, but she managed to keep her hands away from the scar on her chest, if only for a moment. She knew this was an invitation, but for most of her life Livvy had listened instead of speaking. It had always seemed prudent to her, but his engaging grin made her decide that just this once, she would talk without any purpose other than the warmth it brought to her.

He listened.

"Are you asking me if I have any friends, or if I'm a sad girl with a busted heart who sort of lives in her room? Because that would be kind of mean." She grinned at his shock before adding, "It's not true, though. I do love books, and not just because I don't have to run to catch them."

"So you prefer not to run, but you love books." He nodded sagely, as if this had been obvious all along.

"Of course, but that's not because of my heart. No sane person would enjoy running, much like yodeling." She spoke with great certainty, only to have him nod in agreement.

"Naturally. I lost my mind for a moment, forgive me. It must be all the books." He inhaled dramatically, something

Livvy wished she could do, and looked around with great satisfaction. "Every library is different, but books always smell the same no matter where you are."

"They do. And—wow, you're even nerdier than I imagined. I thought I was a rarity."

"You are." His smile faded, replaced with a look that was more adult than his voice.

Blushing, she said, "I *mean* that it makes me feel better knowing there are other people who go around sniffing books."

"Right." He looked at the distant clouds again. His eyes slid from them back to her. They were dark and thoughtful. "I always thought that books could be either a friend or an enemy. It depended on if you wanted to read the truth."

"Don't I know it." There was a bitter turn to her voice, and he looked at her sharply. "I would read everything, trying to find words that told me I was going to live. Everything was always so vague, and I never really found anything specific about me." She sighed. It was a wan sound, but not sad. More like simple acceptance.

"About you? Or your . . . ?" He let his eyes graze the scar, then flicker back to her.

"This, yeah." She touched the raised line, feeling nothing other than slight pressure. The scar was a dead thing hinting at trouble underneath, like the tip of a dangerous rock near a shoreline. "When I was little, it was easy to believe that I was special or something, but then I found out I was in danger. We would go to doctors every week. Always a different face and voice, but always the same sort of thing. I knew—I mean, I could tell that it was hard on mom and dad. They tried to stay the same, always upbeat and acting like *this* was the doctor who would tell me I didn't need a transplant, that it would be okay. I couldn't break their fiction, you know?"

He nodded, slowly. "I do."

She let her head fall to one side, looking up at him. "How?"

"My parents were always hoping that things were going to be different for me, but I knew better. They could listen and help, but they weren't *me*. They weren't inside my shell."

"That's it. I have a shell." Her smile grew wide. "My spirit animal must be a clam. I'm not very fast, I tend to sit in one place, and I always seem to be waiting for the tide to help me out."

"Could be worse. You might be a snail. Can you imagine having to carry your own house around?"

She snorted then covered the lower half of her face with a hand. "Sorry. Caught me just right. I don't even carry a book bag if I can help it."

"I don't blame you. Heavy things are a bother." They watched the river in companionable silence for a moment, but then he grew restless. "You never really answered me. Why books?"

She thought it over, since he seemed to want the truth. "I guess I love to travel. Never had the chance to do the real thing."

His answering look told her he understood. "Yeah, there is that. But what's to say something in your mind isn't as real as anything else?"

She considered that. "Okay, then, yeah. I guess I have done a fair bit of traveling."

"Me too." He plucked a book from the shelf beneath

him. "I'd be stunned if I didn't go somewhere else reading this. Do you feel like that?" He leaned toward her, his eyes bright.

Livvy noticed that the area around them was free of people and very, very quiet. "I do." She paused, letting her heart catch up, then took a bold, deep breath and looked directly at him. She'd never been noticed before, or kissed, or given the gift of someone's complete attention other than her parents.

It was like a drug.

She let herself go just the slightest bit and put one hand over his long fingers. They were warm and still, and for the longest heartbeat of her life, Keiron didn't move.

Then he turned his hand over so gently that she wasn't sure it happened, and their fingers twined together for a second before he smiled, a hesitant grin curling his lips.

"Liv?" he asked, his voice low.

"Yes?" It was, to her credit, not a whisper.

"Can we sit down?" He looked at the floor. The carpet was bland. They would be the only signs of life in it if they were to sit. Wordlessly, they let go with some reluctance and sat, cross-legged and knees touching.

"Okay," she said, and it was a long, drawn-out question in itself. "What next?"

Keiron held up a finger. "A suggestion?"

"I'm all ears." She flipped her ears forward with her fingers. He laughed, then they grew quiet once again. It was still silent. Clouds began to flutter past, casting intermittent shadows on the floor around them, but the sun remained on their shoulders.

He leaned forward to say something, and she fought to keep her eyes open as nerves swept her away into the unknown of the moment. "Tell me more." He was very close. She could feel his breath, and it was sweet.

"Where should I start?" Her voice was ragged with nerves. He took both of her hands in his, and the calming effect was instant.

"How about at the beginning?" It sounded reasonable. They were still close, but she wasn't scared. Not then.

He reached out and traced her scar with the tip of one finger. She flinched, then caught herself. No one had ever done that, not that she would have let them. The ridge of skin was always something to be ignored, like a scarlet letter writ from her cursed imperfection. He looked at the scar, then back to her eyes. They were bright golden in the sun, and he would have believed anything she said just then.

She lifted her chest to inhale, and let it trickle slowly from her as images flickered past her eyes in scenes from a life that seemed far away. "Okay. It isn't pretty, I'm warning you."

When he took his finger away, his hand dropped back to hers. His face was somewhere between hope and wonder. "Yes it is."

CHAPTER TEN:

Cressa

*H*abira arrived with a silken rush of air and descended from the house aerie in long, smooth strides. She was tall, dark, and a perfect blend of Saiinov's stern features leavened by Vasa's beauty. Of all the Skywatchers Cressa had met, Habira was easily the most lethal-looking specimen. Every gesture seemed to be a form of barely controlled violence, although when she greeted her parents her voice was warm and kind.

"This is the Flyer?" Habira said by way of introduction.

Cressa shrank back at the intense scrutiny of dark eyes that pierced her from under the flying cowl worn by Skywatchers. It gave the wearer a martial, raptor-like appearance, but when she stripped it off and walked forward with a hand extended in greeting, her visage was changed into that of an athletic, pretty woman in her late youth. Her hair was the color of storm clouds, bound up in a complex plait held in place by a series of carved ivory pins fashioned from an airbeast of some unknown kind. She wore a single blue gem at her throat, and her flying armor rippled with colorless mystery over a body that was trained for war.

"I won't bite, child." Habira's smile danced between amusement and measure as she determined how she would deal with the messenger bringing news of her family's newfound troubles.

"Thank you, lady," Cressa said in clipped tones. She took note of the fact that no one seemed surprised at Habira's arrival, which could only mean that House Windhook had powerful allies within the council grounds.

Cressa's departure was far from public knowledge, and she knew for a fact that no one had followed her. She had training in that very area, and was naturally paranoid both due to her social status as well as her occupation.

"You know, then?" Saiinov asked, his tone indicating he sought confirmation rather than discussion.

"It was decided only this morning. I'd just arrived from the east, and my wing was disbanding at the armory. The whispers were persistent as I conducted my business before leaving the city." She grinned ruefully at that. Rumors propelled more clouds than the winds, or at least that was the case in the city. The only thing people enjoyed more than war was scandal, and both were possible with news that involved House Windhook.

Saiinov growled, "Who initiated the feint?"

"Feint?" Habira looked dubious. "You think this is cover for some greater act?"

Her father snorted with disgust, causing Vasa to put a hand on his arm, which was rigid with anger. "I think it would be sheer folly to plan for anything less, don't you, dear?" He looked at Vasa to gauge her opinion.

She merely nodded, confirming the suspicion that their plight was anything but an internal familial dispute.

Habira busied herself with a drink, stirring it as she looked out over the roiling clouds. When she spoke it was as an equal, rather than a child. She'd earned that kind of credibility with her parents, a fact that did not go unnoticed by Cressa. "I think that *every* detail of this anomaly must be examined for the benefit of our family." She looked at Cressa pointedly, raising her brows in question at the presence of a council messenger who had been sworn to deliver a virtual declaration of war.

"She is welcome." Vasa pointed to the shading of Cressa's feathers with a gesture of finality. "Everyone in this room has something to lose if the council is left unchecked."

Habira considered that, then sat down opposite Cressa and tilted her head as she measured the young woman. "You're a Blightwing." It was an invitation, not a slur. After a pause that lengthened like the shadows at day's end, it became apparent that no one would speak until Cressa, so she cleared her throat and waved helplessly.

"I—yes, I am. And I'm guilty." The reply was terse, factual. It was clearly something Cressa had not discussed recently, if at all. Silence continued until Saiinov stirred, uncrossing his legs and leaning forward to affix her with a look of such interest it made her squirm.

He opened a palm to her, saying, "It would appear my daughter wishes to understand you better, and I never doubt her instincts. If you please, your crime? How did you come to be stained by the sin of murdering one's own blood?"

The wind whistled past outside, a high keening of relentless motion that only made Cressa wish ever more that she were in a current on her way to somewhere else, but she fought that urge, settled in, and organized her words.

"I have been in service to the council for less than a month. In fact, this is only the third time I've gone far from the city on official business. I've been in and around Sliver for most of my flights."

"A month? I've heard nothing of a crime that would have caused you to be branded —" Saiinov began, but Vasa stilled him with a gaze. Sometimes marriage meant not saying anything at all.

"You wouldn't have, because it didn't happen here. It was in the east, and word might never reach here, let alone House Windhook. In my month of service, I've learned that the council, ah, *edits* the truth for people who are outside their direct control. You fall among that class, no disrespect intended." She smiled apologetically at her brash report, but they wanted the truth, so that was what she would deliver.

Habira looked on with great interest. "A question, and you may choose not to answer, although I confess to a burning curiosity. Who did you kill?"

The air left the room with those words, and nothing moved except Cressa's hands, which twined around each other like nervous serpents. She lifted her eyes from the expanse of floor, taking in the powerful family around her and forming the truth as she knew it, for a simple answer would not be enough. "House Carillon is — I mean, it *was* in the Eastern Reaches. Do you know what the most important thing is to a family from the east?" To her credit, the question sounded casual, even conversational.

Habira answered immediately. "Their title. It's generational, and it can go to a son or daughter; all that matters is that they are the strongest."

"That's partially true, but you wouldn't know the details. Not unless you live in an eastern family, and preferably one that has existed for more than three generations." Cressa leaned forward, her brow a thundercloud of violent memories. "As the family continues, the title gains value."

Saiinov snorted. "Obviously."

Cressa shook her head, indicating he wasn't grasping the nuance of eastern hierarchies. The east wasn't just distant, it was alien when compared to the west and the lands of the Crescent Council. "No, not like that. Of course the longer a name exists, it carries more weight, but our traditions are different. Here, you might even call our ways mercenary."

Vasa snapped her fingers in understanding. "You can purchase the title to a house? It isn't granted or earned?" Her voice oozed disbelief, confirming Cressa's suspicions. Their ways were too different to be fully compatible. It was only distance and the council that brought them together, and even then she suspected that the distance was ultimately a good thing. Wars had been started over far more trivial matters than the right of succession to a powerful family name.

"Yes, but only if there's no one capable of refuting the attempting purchase. If a family has members who are weak, or too old, or disinterested, then the changing of leadership can result in one or more suitors attempting to usurp the authority of the living family members. Sometimes, the results are horrible." She'd seen a family hurled to their doom from a house simply because they were too young to resist a local power grab. No one cared save the dying, and the incident was soon forgotten, chalked up to the brutal realities of eastern politics.

Saiinov gave her a measured look. "You seem quite capable to me, even at your age. I take it that someone in your family had no interest in ceding control of the house to you? Or is there something even less savory at the heart of your crime?"

"Something like that, sir." Cressa stood, unfastening the central ridge of her thin, flowing armor. She peeled back the silver scales to reveal a flat stomach rippling with muscle. It would have been perfect if not for the jagged, angry scar that ran under her ribs and terminated in a wicked upward turn just under her heart.

Vasa inhaled, the sound of a mother who has seen evidence of a child being badly hurt. "Gods of air, who did that?" She reached out instinctively toward the scar, but withdrew her hand out of courtesy and shame at her reaction.

"My eldest sister. She was a vain, shallow woman who wanted nothing more than to sell our title, and home, and everything that had been curated over time." She shook her head sadly, thinking of the bitter woman she felt only contempt for now. "I alone could challenge her after the death of our parents, so I did."

"By legal combat?" Habira's question had the tone of someone who knew violence as a means to solving problems.

"It never got that far. She tried to remove me by force, but I fought back. I suspected her of treachery, but even that was — I wasn't ready. I never thought of my own family conspiring against me with violence. I was a child. I still am, if you want to know the truth." Her sheepish admission made her seem even younger, but when she began speaking there was iron in her voice. "Belora, my sister; she wasn't alone."

"A lover?" Saiinov asked, his cynical snort describing what he thought of Belora and her actions.

"I think so. He was a bit older, but he seemed quite ragged. His tunic was faded, but it had once been that of an eastern guard. Belora certainly welcomed him into our home." She shivered with a memory. "She said nothing when he grabbed me, and I knew. Up until then, I thought she was just greedy and stupid. I didn't know she was willing to go that far."

"Far enough to kill?" Habira asked, again in that professionally curious tone.

Cressa merely nodded. "He started dragging me to the aerie, and they didn't even pretend that it was anything other than murder. Belora wrapped me with a cord, but she forgot to search me. It was her last mistake."

"You were armed? And you killed her then?" Vasa asked, he words gentle. She surmised Cressa was no habitual murderer.

"Always." Cressa twisted her wrist and a bone blade appeared in her hand like a wraith. "From the first predator I ever killed. I whittled it over a span of weeks until it fit my hand perfectly, and then I wrapped the handle in down from a Windbeast who nested near our home." The stiletto was thin, pale, and wicked. She held it with an ease that spoke to a long relationship, and Habira nodded approvingly, as did Saiinov.

Vasa looked inscrutable, her thoughts hidden from the child who was proving to be more complicated and dangerous than a simple messenger.

"What happened to your House?" Habira's question

arrowed through the building silence.

Cressa shrugged, indifferent to a fate that was well past, but she humored them. "The same thing that always happens to the weaker houses. We were split up, stolen, our personal things taken as payment for my crime, or given as favors to friends of the council. Soon, I was left with only one option." She looked at herself and nodded, as if reconfirming her status. "I took it."

The wind whistled for some time before anyone spoke again, and it was Saiinov whose growl interrupted the quiet. "You had no one willing to champion you before the council?" Every word dripped with disgust at this insult to Cressa, despite their inauspicious beginning. Above all else, Saiinov detested the machinations of the council when it gutted innocent victims. Cressa was no more deserving of her sister's shortcomings than she was the curse of being known as a Blightwing, no matter what she admitted to doing.

Vasa looked on, her maternal nerves roaring in protest at what the council had wrought. Habira's eyes were filmed with a murderous glaze. She'd always been quickest to anger, but then she was nearly as lethal as Saiinov. She could afford the odd impetuous outburst.

"When you were bonded into service, did the council explain all of the details? Are you aware of the law as it stands?" Vasa probed. She was beyond quick-witted; for her, all problems could be solved if given enough time and consideration. She was clearly looking downwind at the issues of Garrick and Cressa, and she saw an intersection in the distance. To Vasa, that was something to be exploited.

"I — I think so. I mean, I know that I am bound for life, or until I can balance my crime in the eyes of the council."

Cressa smiled, a wry gesture that was far too old for her features. "I'm told that sort of thing is rare."

Habira snorted. "Try never. Or impossible. The council exists solely to further their own ends, which are beyond Gordian. They don't even tell one another what their plans are, let alone the unwashed masses outside the walls of Sliver." She pointed toward the hallowed space of the council city, but it wasn't visible from House Windhook. That was most likely best, for Sliver, as the council called their home, claimed dominion over all that they could see from their aerie. Inhabitants who disagreed with their sovereign viewpoint were greeted with a flurry of wings, weapons, and brutality until they changed their minds and took a knee before the five men and women to whom power was the purest drug of all.

"I know. I have to hope, though." Cressa's admission was heartbreaking in its simplicity. She was alone, branded as a monster, and looking forward to a life of servitude and death, which was why Saiinov's next words were no surprise at all.

He stood as a look passed between him and Vasa. "Flyer Cressa. I submit to your command for an appearance, as does my wife and daughter. We will not yield our remaining children, nor may the council or its agents enter House Windhook without fatal repercussions." He raised his voice and looked upward, addressing the elemental of the house. "Hear and witness the command of this family, Windhook. You are to disable or kill anyone not of this bloodline. There are to be no warnings given, and no quarter offered in the event they try to take this house by force. Is this understood?"

A stentorian voice rushed toward them from all

directions at once. "Heard and recorded. This day will be marked, and I will remain vigilant until ordered otherwise."

"Thank you." Saiinov bowed respectfully in the direction of the sky. Cressa's eyes were like saucers. He looked at the young woman, noting her disbelief. "Your home had no elemental in command?"

"No. I thought—I never knew they tolerated the company of others." Her voice dropped to a stage whisper. "He *lives* here?"

Vasa's warm laugh filled the space around them. Even Habira chuckled, if briefly. "It might be more accurate to say we live in him, although that isn't entirely true either. But rest assured, House Windhook will remain safe until our return from enemy lands."

"We're just going to Sliver, aren't we?" Cressa looked about, confused.

Saiinov stood, his face a mask of growing anger. "We are, and it is most certainly the lair of our enemies. I would hardly call it anything other than a place of hostility."

Habira was already in motion. "We'll need—"

"Everything. Bring everything for of the possible outcomes once we answer the petition of the council. You know it can go in three directions. It seems only prudent to plan for them to strike at us where we're weakest." Vasa began her own movement, a series of decisive steps that took her toward her work areas. "We'll send word to the children that they are not to approach Sliver until this is finished."

"I'll do that." Habira readied messages in her neat, block lettering. When she'd completed the small stack of shells, she ascended to swirling stairs that led to the exterior alcove of the aerie. Pursing her lips, she emitted a high three-note trill that rose and fell like a mournful whistle in the distance. After a short wait, dark shadows began to descend through the growing gloom of night. They moved like ribbons in water, smooth, unhurried, and silent. One by one, Habira held the messages aloft to the passing Airdancers, their undulations never ceasing as they placed wet, rubbery mouths around the message shells and flowed off into the night, their sides glowing delicately with coded messages for their brethren.

"You have Airdancers on call?" Cressa's shock was nearly at a fever pitch. To partner with an elemental was unheard of, but to have the ability to summon Airdancers at an instant was power like she'd never seen before. *Who are these people?* Her moment of disbelief was followed by shame at having arrived with such an imperious attitude. She felt lucky they hadn't clipped her and sent her spiraling into the unending brightness for her impertinence.

"Naturally. It's only prudent if you don't wish to spend your days in the sky sending messages," Habira replied amiably, before realizing the unintended slight to Cressa. "My apology. I meant no offense, especially given your personal journey." Her face reddened slightly, but Cressa merely inclined her head in acceptance.

"It is rather a waste of a good flight to spend it hurrying from one place to another. I don't enjoy the scenery as I should, but still" — she looked wistfully into the rusty sunset where the Airdancers had vanished on their tasks — "I should probably ride a thermal now and then. It might make some of the days less grim." Just then, she didn't sound like a young woman. She had the ring of defeat in her voice. It was an unnatural, and slightly bitter undertone that aged her beyond her years. It seemed that in her heart, Cressa was a practical soul, which made squandering her life in pointless servitude even less palatable.

The bustle began to die as Saiinov appeared before Cressa, an expectant look on his face. "You'll join us, of course? I wouldn't care to think of you covering that much sky at night."

"And alone. I don't care if you're a messenger, it's too dangerous," added Habira, while pulling on thin gloves made of an unknown skin. They had pads sewn into the palms and the look of being well-used.

"I . . . will?" Cressa asked, uncertain what the family intended her to do. They couldn't move the entire house, not on short notice, so there was clearly something else in the near future.

Vasa recognized her confusion, smiling gently. "This way, then. I forgot, you're originally an easterner. This might be a bit different for you." She guided Cressa along as the family descended a stairwell that had been hidden by wafting curtains. After two full turns, they emerged into the winds on a platform beneath House Windhook. A light, rhythmic thumping met Cressa's ears. It was near full dark as the last sinuous strands of rosy glow began to die away. The sun was setting, and the night wrapped them in cool mystery before their eyes could adjust.

"Step carefully, please." Saiinov held a lamp aloft, the circle of buttery light casting down onto the deck of a small windship that bobbed obediently at the platform. It was narrow, long, and sported four equidistant masts that curved back like scimitars. Each part of the craft appeared to be carved from the bones of a Windbeast so large that it boggled the imagination. With practiced ease, the three members of House Windhook began untying sails that fluttered into place with a cheerful snapping before filling with the steady wind and dragging the ship outward toward the stars.

"An airship?" Cressa nearly whispered, but Habira heard the confused oath from her position at the steering column. She looked fully at ease holding the twin paddles that controlled the pitch and yaw, her feet busily working unseen pedals to send the craft into a brisk turn to the east.

"Of course. Most houses have them. Why would you think us any different?" Saiinov asked in a patient voice.

Cressa stumbled over her reply. "I—I just thought since I was delivering a summons, that—well, I don't know what to think." She exhaled with frustration at her inability to relate the previous places she'd been. Most were run down or on the verge of implosion due to familial conflict. House Windhook was something entirely different. They had power, and wealth, and relationships with the creatures of the sky that verged into myth. *The council may have taken too large a bite with this family*, thought Cressa. The possibility of that august body being taken to task gave her a thrill that ran the length of her spine. Of all the places she'd been, this family was the one group who didn't seem the slightest bit fearful of a confrontation.

In fact, they were sailing toward it with all haste.

"We'll be in the air until morning, at least. Sleep if you can, Cressa," came the kindly suggestion from Vasa. Her serene face was turned into the wind, a cloak pulled around her like a mother's caress. The colored fabric rippled under the gleam of stars that wheeled overhead, their radiant light broken only by occasional feathery clouds that streamed back toward the west.

"My thanks, lady, but shouldn't I be awake when I bring my prisoners in?" Cressa's slow smile gleamed in the night. Her clever rejoinder brought a laugh from the entire Windhook family, but only Vasa replied to the young woman.

The lady's voice was a rich lilting note among the steady song of the wind. "We'll be certain to wake you prior to our arrival. It wouldn't do to have you seen as sleeping on the job." Vasa waved a hand at Cressa, indicating she should lean back and get what rest was possible while they hurtled through the night. It was a generous thing, but well in line with the character of what Cressa had seen of this powerful, mysterious family. She positioned herself as well as the surroundings would permit, listening to the subtle creak of sail and wind, and before she could even consider anything else, she slept.

CHAPTER ELEVEN:

Thursday

*A*t some point, the clouds in the distance went from far to near. A brooding wall of gray was slowly approaching, hungrily eating the broad rays of the sun and causing the day to be cooler, dimmer, and a bit sad.

Livvy sat in the breakroom, sipping listlessly at her drink. There was nothing about the space around her that could inspire anything other than a shrug. Impersonal tan cabinets ran around three walls, their contents unknown to Livvy because she didn't paw through them looking feverishly for coffee filters or other items needed by the early staff. A microwave sat in one corner, reeking of burnt popcorn, its digital numbers pulsing in an aggressive red tone. There were two vending machines with an array of small, overpriced bags of salty things; none of them interested her, so she sat in a plastic chair looking at a poster that was comically inept as only public service announcements can be. *Reading: Get in the Game!* read the poster, covered with children dressed up for various sports. Their haircuts were out of date, just like the clothing, and they all held a book aloft in one hand as if they'd just freed the sword Excalibur. She smiled and looked down at the scarred table, wondering if Keiron would be waiting for her when she returned to her desk.

That thought was almost enough for her to get up and leave, but she knew that excitement led to being short of breath, so she calmed herself by closing her eyes and counting slowly backward from one hundred. She was at ninety-one when the woman's voice broke into her reverie like a wailing siren.

"You're the new girl who can't walk around too fast, aren't you?"

Livvy turned with a mix of surprise and irritation. She couldn't understand how the woman had been sitting there all along, but it made sense. When she was out of breath, the world faded away; even things that were close enough to touch. "I — yes?"

"You are, or you aren't?" She was painfully thin, with frizzy hair and enormous black eyes that hung in the sockets like dark coals. Her smile was painful to see; lips that had been thin to begin with were pulled back over long, yellowed teeth. A battered coffee cup sat before her, wrapped in her long fingers. She could have been anywhere from forty to seventy, but Livvy suspected she was merely young and had lived a hard life.

"I am. I work at the desk. Are you . . .?" Livvy let the question trail off, hoping for an answer without any awkward interrogation. There was something almost hungry about the woman, who responded to her question by taking a long swallow of coffee.

"Klara Holo, I'm sorry. I can be a bit spacey around lunchtime." Her smile deepened into something warmer, and there was a hint of an accent that gave her words a musical lilt.

Livvy felt her chest loosen in relief. Confrontation wasn't her thing, and up until that moment the break room had been a sort of haven. "I love your name. And yeah, I get dreamy when I need a snack. Mom always said that she could tell how hungry I was by how vague I was talking."

Klara laughed; it was a dry sound, but not unkind. "I know. Sorry about sneaking up on you, sort of. You had your eyes closed for a long time. Are you alright?" She looked worried. It was an expression Livvy knew well. People almost always looked worried when they spoke to her, as if she were made of glass and falling to the floor. It was exhausting.

"I'm okay. Just got a little tired. Happens a lot." She grinned as a gentle way to close the line of questions, before asking her own. "Where do you work? I don't think I've seen you, but I'm not all over the place, exactly."

"Do you stay at the desk?" Klara returned her volley, looking interested.

"Mostly. I have a medical thing; it makes it hard to get around. So I sort of stay there. Or here. Usually one or the other, or in between."

"Mmm. Oh, and yeah, I work here. Sorry, wasn't dodging you. I work as an assistant to Miss Henatis, usually two or three days a week. You been here long?" Klara stood to refill her mug. She appeared to like coffee the way Livvy liked pizza. That is, constantly and with a permanent refill.

"This is my first week. I'm still sort of learning what to do. And not do." Livvy's tone was so careful, Klara laughed.

"She can be a lot to take, but she's not inherently evil

or anything." Klara laughed, displaying all kinds of teeth in an awkward, braying series of wheezes. "Honestly, as long as you follow certain rules, you're gonna be okay."

"Like what? I mean, I want to keep my job. I guess I'm not really sure what Miss Henatis wants from me." Livvy shrugged, a summation of everything she didn't know about the library and the policies of one Teresa Henatis.

Klara smiled, then lifted a hand. "There are rules outside the rules, that's what you're really asking me, isn't it?" At Livvy's nod, she went on. "Right, so the most important thing is to never go in her office unless she calls you. That's probably more important than all the other rules combined."

"I wouldn't dream of it," Livvy said, and she meant it. "But, um — why? Other than the obvious." She thought of manners, and decorum, and lots of other words that meant the same thing: Don't be rude.

"Well, you know that we have a lot of rare books?" Klara raised a thin brow; even the hair on her face looked tired and kind of worn out.

"We do?" Livvy knew little beyond her desk and what Dozer had shown her.

"Quite a few, and they're valuable. Anyway, all of them are in her office. She has a security lock on the shelves, so she's extra touchy about people being in their without her. It's kind of her sanctuary, so she keeps it under lock and key." She looked thoughtful before adding, "Also, they're worth a lot of money, I think. She has lists and maps and all of the old things that libraries tend to collect over the years. It's pretty impressive."

"You've seen it?" Livvy asked.

"Once or twice. I don't linger because you can't eat a

book. I tend to spend my breaks in here." Klara lifted her mug with an impish grin. It made her look slightly younger, but not much.

"Okay, I'll avoid the inner sanctum. What else?" Livvy's smile broke out at the thought of Miss Henatis in a wizard's robe, muttering over a table crammed with skulls and other arcana. It would be an improvement over the severe figure she cut on a daily basis.

"Well, I wouldn't eat at Frankly, Frank's, no matter what, and I would avoid getting too cozy with the regulars." She grimaced. It looked more natural than her earlier smile, a fact that Livvy found unsettling.

"I tried, and couldn't, but I'll keep it in mind." The taste of chemicals and plastic came rushing back like an unwelcome guest. She swallowed carefully before speaking again. The saliva flooding her mouth tasted like a rubber hose. Not that she'd eaten many, but still. She could guess. "Why not the regulars? They seem harmless." And they did. She found their fussing and routine to be comforting.

"Oh, they certainly look harmless, but you don't want to be around them in a group. They tend to be a bit combative."

"What? Danny? Miss Willie? Fighting?" Livvy was incredulous. Of *all* the terms she might use for her regulars, combative was dead last. They were quirky readers, and nothing more.

Klara waved, partially admitting her miscue. "Well, okay. Maybe not in the way it sounded, but they can be pushy. Just watch out for yourself. You don't want them shoving you around, is all." She sniffed as a way to express her doubt that Livvy could understand anything about the world of adults.

Livvy knew that noise; she'd heard it for years from doctors who did everything but roll their eyes at her when she dared to ask them a question. Her conversations were usually held while a nurse was plunging a needle into some soft part of her, so she felt justified in asking what was happening and why. Klara might have thought she was protecting Livvy from something outside her experience, but she was wrong. In seventeen years, Livvy had experienced everything that life had offer, good and bad. She was sometimes timid, but not by nature. Her quiet times were driven by necessity, not uncertainty or fear, and her skin was thick enough not to fear the consequences of standing up for herself.

Other than her parents, who else would? It was a question she mulled during the long nights when she lay under the glowing stars of her ceiling at home. Her dad put the stickers up when she was a little girl, telling her that she couldn't go to the stars, but he would bring the stars to her. She remembered him pointing to the constellations glowing softly on the stippled drywall overhead, and thought that in that moment she knew what it meant to have someone care for everything that happened to you, good or bad. Tears pricked her eyes at the thought of — what? Being six years old again? The lumpy feel of her special pillow? Both had been gone for a long time, many years and surgeries ago. With each successive cut under the surgeon's knives, she knew that she left something behind, and it wasn't just a pillow with grape juice stains or a stuffed turtle with a hat at a jaunty angle. Livvy was leaving herself behind, bit by bit, and she knew that if a heart did not find her, one time, under the care of those surgeons, she wouldn't wake up.

"Honey? You still with us?" Klara's voice jolted her back to the present and the austere feel of the break room.

"Umm, yeah. Sorry. Lost in my head for a moment." Livvy put her hand on the scar that ran up her chest; it was a defensive motion she used to fend off further questions or unwanted attention. When people saw the poor, frail girl nervously massaging a massive scar, they backed off out of respect. Klara was no different, although her eyes did linger on the scar with something quite different than curiosity. "So, thanks. I won't go into Miss Henatis' office unless she, I don't know, tells me my life depends on it or something."

Klara smiled, a thin, dry event that made her age return in a flurry of wrinkles and shadowed creases. When she spoke, her voice was low. "It just might. She's not to be trifled with." With that, she stood and left Livvy to have the room, alone except for the hum of a fluorescent tube that flickered occasionally. The refrigerator clicked and began a low, obedient hum, but other than that the room was oppressively still.

"I need to get out of here." Livvy's voice echoed slightly, adding to the sense of desolation in the room.

"I agree. You should help me with my research." Keiron leaned in the doorway, a smile playing at his lips.

The first thing Livvy noticed was that there was no guile about him; he looked and acted happy to see her.

A smile crackled across her face at his arrival. "Really? What kind of research? Something critical and world-saving, I hope?"

He raised a hand solemnly. "It is. I seek to find the secrets of nothing less than a lost empire." His grin broke through like the sun in clouds, and Livvy giggled, a noise she hated making. It was girlish and small, she thought, but

Keiron took her hand and pulled her to standing. "You shouldn't be afraid of laughing. It's nice to hear."

Mollified, she let herself look up into his eyes. There was no taunting, none of the mean spirit she'd come to expect. His face was tilted down, the smile lingering. The light overhead gave off an inopportune pop, breaking the moment. "I can help you find your lost people, as long as we don't have to dig. I'm not that good with a shovel."

"That makes two of us. I'd rather look in books. Show me?" He began guiding her to the door, then out into the wider world of the second floor.

"Why the sudden interest in — what are we looking for?" She paused, waiting to decide on their direction based on his request. Steps and time were two things she wouldn't waste, especially with him.

"It's a place, really. I guess you'd call it a city state, or something. A family who fought an empire so that they could remain free." They were standing in front of a massive book case, its shelves groaning with volumes that looked heavy and important. Keiron ran a finger idly over the spines of a series titled *War and Struggle in the Western Empire.* "This seems like a good place to start. They *are* in the east, after all."

"Are or were? Big difference. If we want ancient history, we have to go over there, but if it's something current, we might be in the right place. Do you have a name? A place?" She held her finger out, pointing randomly at the rows of books. Their spines and dustjackets were like a kaleidoscope of color and words, running brightly into the distance.

"House Windhook." His answer was short, definitive.

Livvy's brow furrowed at the answer. It was an exotic

name, and nothing she'd ever heard before. Maybe it was something for advanced senior year history, but up until that moment Livvy had never heard those three words put together at once.

"Where is it? Or, was it?" Her curiosity prickled at the new thing. She loved learning of anything that was beyond her own horizons, which was most of the known world.

"In the west, but I don't know if it's still in existence. They were involved in a war with a body of tyrants known as the Crescent Council. Does that help?" He shrugged slightly, powerless to understand the nature of the library.

"It's not a bad place to start. Let's go over here." They moved off together, taking a left, and another left. When they stood in front of the reference section, Livvy began running her fingers over the big, plain books, her lips moving silently as she read and discarded titles. After a long moment, she brightened, pointing at an enormous blue and silver book that sat on the highest shelf. It was alone save one other title, a companion volume if she was guessing, although that one was an angry red with silver lettering. "Bring that big guy down for me, will you? I think we might start here."

Kieron reached up and effortlessly plucked the massive book from its resting place; the dust that sprinkled into the weak sunbeam from a nearby window meant that they were the first people to remove it in some time.

He wiped the cover with a theatrical cough before putting it down on the nearest table with a dull thud. "There must be a *lot* of history in that book. Hope it's worth it." His grin was rueful.

"It is. There's no such thing as a bad book." Livvy loved books and found comfort in them. They brought the world to her when her heart would not let her travel. There was no restriction on her imagination; not even with a chest that was too quiet by half. "Let's see what we have here. House Windhook, you say? So they were like Sparta, or Carthage or something?"

"Exactly, but with less people. The Crescent Council was bigger, but only because they had a lot of people living around them. Sort of like a support staff, except they couldn't really leave Sliver if they wanted to. The council was too powerful to let people go, or at least that's what I think."

"Well, then let's find out what the author thinks." She looked at the cover. *V. Windhook*, read the embossed golden letters. "Well, I think we found them." She opened the cover with a light creak. It was heavy, bound in leather, and ridged with gold highlights that flickered under the sunlight spilling across the table, but then the encroaching clouds snuffed out the last of the light and the table fell into the harsh glow of the overhead lights. "What do we want to know?" She smiled at him expectantly.

"Everything."

Flipping a page, she marveled at the paper's heft. It felt old, and her touch was reverent. She looked sideways at Keiron before asking the question he had quietly avoided since bringing the book down from its aerie. "Why?"

Livvy was an expert in being lied to. Doctors lied to her about whether or not a procedure would hurt, or if she would feel like dying from the pain, or a thousand other reasons that people found to lie to her. Keiron did not, for a second, think about lying. But he did think, and that was long enough for Livvy to go on high alert, wondering what he might say.

"Call it a family interest. Also, I sort of already got what I wanted." His eyes were fixed on the pages, but she sensed he was watching her.

"Really?" She leaned away from him to get a wider view. "Do tell." At that, she put both hands under her chin and fluttered her eyes until he snorted with laughter.

"Okay, right. But it's true." He took her hand and squeezed it lightly. *Lup lup lup*. Her heart galloped ahead, eager to see what was over the hill with Keiron at her side. She felt spots of color on her cheeks, and realized that it was incredibly quiet in their little alcove. For the rest of the world, they were untouchable. The thought thrilled and scared her, and she liked it.

"What do you want?" Her eyes fired from within with golden flecks in the lingering afternoon sun. Dust motes ringed her in a slow dance, the currents of air nearly still in their silent harbor. It was a direct, even brutal question, but he chose to answer, and Livvy felt them moving toward each other in a swirl, just like the brilliant bits of dust that were too busy catching light to notice the inevitable attraction of the two people beneath them.

"I would like to know everything that's in that book," he said, watching her master the crestfallen look that flashed across her face. His fingers twined with hers, slowly.

She didn't pull back. She couldn't, not if she was being honest.

"I also want to kiss you." He considered that, realizing that his priorities were not in the proper order. Not with a girl like Livvy. "I want the kiss more, though. Much more."

"I'll think about it." That was a lie. She didn't need to think about it; kissing him had been on her mind since their first meeting, but she wasn't going to give him the high ground without a fight.

Not yet.

Her words brought clouds to his eyes, and she relented, but only just. With a challenging slowness, she raised one brow and looked at him. Invitation hung in the air between them, thick and unspoken. He leaned down as her eyes closed. She could feel the warmth of his breath, sweet and new to her senses in every way. There was a sly tingle as their lips grew closer, like the announcement of a distant storm.

And then it happened. It was lightning wrapped in velvet, a growing heat rushing through them as their lips met and Livvy reached up to hold him, letting go of all her fears in that simple, soft, living moment of celebration. It was something so real that she felt her heart leap upward as it struggled to keep up with her wave of happiness. When they pulled apart, their hands lingered, fingers entwined like reeds in a basket. His eyes were open with amazement. Hers were bright with joy, and they savored the moment, only drawing apart so that there would be more distance between them before the next kiss. They both decided without words that a longer approach would make the moment even sweeter, and anticipation would only draw them closer together faster and with more desire.

The second kiss was better still. Livvy pulled him to her before caution pushed them apart, reluctant but giddy with heat. Their smiles were a mirror; each the perfect reflection of their marvel at discovering each other. She leaned her forehead against his shoulder, and it fit.

"Of course it would," she murmured, and he didn't have to ask what she meant. He knew. When she looked up at him after a long moment, his grin was gone, replaced by open admiration. He *saw* her. It was just as she'd hoped, and more than he'd wanted. She wasn't the girl who'd been born with a broken heart, she was real, and she was holding his hands as if her life depended on it.

In a way, it did.

Keiron knew that for Livvy to survive, she would have to be willing to live at any cost, and that meant she was going to endure yet another surgery. He needed her to be at ease, so he pulled the enormous book between them, breaking the moment with a rueful grin. With one hand, he flipped it open, revealing a map, but he quickly went past the sepia-lined shape of a forgotten land, stopping when he got to the table of contents.

"This is what I was looking for." He stifled a laugh at her cool look, then kissed her hand quickly to silence any protest. "I know. You're more important than the book, but I didn't exactly expect all this to happen, you know."

"All this?" She narrowed her eyes, but there was a smile playing at her lips.

"Yeah, just — well, I would much rather walk down by the river with you and watch the ducks, but instead I do want to read this as long as we've found it. Maybe after a bit, we can catch the best part of the afternoon? Down there, I mean?" He looked askance at the broad river winding away past the windows. It was smooth, even serene. It looked utterly still, save for the occasional flotsam going downriver at a sedate pace.

"Fair enough. I can't promise I'll be up for it, but this is nice too." She looked around at their alcove, savoring the quiet.

"It is." He squeezed her hand once, and it seemed that

in that second, they became a pair. Moments earlier, it had been Livvy, the girl with scars, and Keiron, the boy with questions. Now, they held each other with a newfound delicacy that showed no signs of stopping. The air in the alcove remained electric, but took on a less fevered tone as both of them felt the fear of a moment gone wrong beginning to fade. There were no mistakes between them, only possibilities.

So, a pair. Their knees touched gently as Keiron looked down at the massive book, its pages an expanse of antique white filled to bursting with print that had faded over time. With a grin, he split his focus between the book and Livvy.

"The Crescent Council seems like a nice bunch of people, if you're into that sort of thing." He flipped through the first pages, his eyes flickering over the columns of type.

"What sort of thing?" Livvy looked at the pages with interest. Whoever had written the book had done so with great care. There was a sense of time and order to each page as Keiron turned past them.

"Ruling with an iron fist, waging war without care, bleeding people of their life's work, stuff like that." He grimaced at a new chapter titled *Subject States in the East*, before closing the book with a pronounced thump. "Several hundred pages of a small group of people behaving very badly, if I'm any good at guessing. They certainly do like to throw their weight around."

"Where were these people? I've never heard of them." Livvy looked thoughtful, as many of the charts and names in the book had been completely unknown to her.

"Um, well." Keiron opened the book again, flattening a page that had a beautiful map in dark brown and sepia lines. "Sliver, the seat of power, is in the middle. Duh. The East appears to be" — he waved vaguely — "in the east, so no help there. This might surprise you, but the West is actually — "

"In the west? Got it. So these people weren't exactly fans of flowery language." She narrowed her eyes at him, head tilted in a vaguely predatory manner. The effects of two kisses looked good on Livvy. What had been inside her was now on the outside as well, and she wore it like a birthright. "Why are we reading a moldy book about an empire that may or may not have existed? Is this the part where you tell me you're a prince, and that you need my help to claim your castle?"

He let the silence stretch between them until it fell apart of its own weight, answering her with a nervous smile. "Something like that."

CHAPTER TWELVE:

Sliver

*C*ressa woke to the subtle thump of their arrival at the city docks, long floating piers of hollow wood that stretched hungrily into the dawning sky. There were dozens if not hundreds of airships at other piers; their shapes as varied as the people who moved around them. Dangerous looking daggerships bobbed at the largest moorings, their hulls watched by big, capable-looking soldiers with swords and maces at the ready. The sun threw golden shadows everywhere, muted only by the sprawling sails that rippled in the light morning breezes. Every time Cressa saw Sliver, she felt small. The city was enormous, and shaped like a stylized pair of cupped hands that sprouted towers, high and thin, crowding so closely together they resembled an unruly crop of hair. At the top of each tower snapped a flag, declaring the patronage of Houses both large and small. As the set of power, only the foolish or the strong ignored the importance of Sliver, which made Cressa wonder yet again at exactly *who* the people of House Windhook really were.

There were cries of merchants and the complaints of citizens in a growing volume as the day began in earnest. Saiinov and Vasa were unaffected by all of it, and to Cressa's utter shock Habira was sleeping on the deck, a half smile on her face as she snored lightly. All three had changed clothes during the night; they now wore the formal blue-and-silver of House Windhook, and resembled nothing so much as a trio of warriors with whom an engagement would most certainly be fatal.

The council will see them and reconsider. It is the only possible solution to avoid bloodshed in the city. Cressa's thoughts were darkened further by the total disdain as Habira leapt to her feet, laughing and whistling at a wine merchant who labored under a generous cask on one shoulder. After a brief discussion and purchase, they all stood, sipping something that tasted like sunshine and wind drops, a wine of such astounding clarity that Cressa wasn't totally sure it was even in her glass.

"To diplomacy!" Vasa said, her laughter ringing in the air. They all drank, then stepped delicately onto the docks, which swayed lightly under their feet. As one, the family of Windhook adjusted their dress and adopted an expression so severe that Cressa began to fear for her own safety despite the implied protection of her rank. "You need fear us not at all, Flyer. We are merely preparing to enter the city, and above all else we must present a unified front. I'm afraid that for all their talk of brotherhood and honor, Sliver is ripe with deceit. From here on out, we have one goal only."

"What is that, lady?" Cressa asked only because she could discern nothing from the flat expression Vasa pasted to her normally serene features.

Habira interrupted, a hand curling easily around her sword pommel. "Protect the freedom of Windhook at all costs."

"Bu-but, your son?" Cressa sputtered. She was aghast at the dismissal of a threat to their child, even if she privately thought he was lucky to be a member of that family. His character seemed a wan impersonation of what she'd seen from the other members of Windhook thus far.

Vasa waved an elegant hand in dismissal. "A sideshow. The real issue here is bringing Windhook to heel, and doing so in as public a manner as possible. We will not allow that to happen, just as we forbid the council from punishing our son for something which they cannot grasp."

Saiinov's face was hardened by a will hewn from his desires as a father, husband, and leader. Habira seemed to be in a predatory crouch, and Vasa was on the edge of laughter. Cressa uttered a nervous laugh before adjusting her wings and pointing with what authority she could manage. "I'm to direct you to the anterior hall by way of introduction. I was told, and with some force, that I was to do this immediately upon our arrival."

As one, House Windhook nodded, but it was Saiinov who spoke. "We respect that decision, and the rank commensurate with your station, Flyer Cressa, but must regretfully decline such a request until after we've visited our aerie and left the dust of travel behind us. Besides, it would be considered a slight to the council if we were to appear in a disheveled state."

Cressa regarded their impeccable clothing and knew she was not going to convince them to obey her no matter what. There were other issues at play, ones well beyond her understanding. The council would have to understand. As a Blightwing, she was limited in her powers of persuasion. As a Flyer, she was an underling, and nothing more.

She made her last gambit to them out of fear and desperation. Addressing Vasa, she adopted a respectful tone, her eyes and voice steady. "Lady, may I at least accompany you to your aerie?"

Saiinov's laugh interrupted the momentary tension, and Cressa thought it the most welcome sound of her young life. "Take mercy on the child, Vasa. She's petrified." He put a companionable hand on Cressa's wing, smiling all the while. "We won't make you report emptyhanded, Cressa. You may come with us, although I confess that it might be many hours before we're ready to address the council. Can you stand to wait, even if it's in relative comfort? There might be an unforeseen cost to you, given our status."

Cressa looked at her own wings with a sour twist of her mouth.

"Point taken. Follow us, then. We have a great deal to do." Saiinov waited for Cressa, who fell in behind Vasa.

Habira led with her chin, every motion a challenge to the passersby on the broad, crowded pathway. There was little poverty in Sliver, but even in a land of plenty there were opportunists. Three of them fell in behind the family before they had even cleared the docks. The men moved like wraiths, fading into the crowd at each turn, but always edging forward in an attempt to bracket Habira, who was a few paces ahead, her cloak pulled up to cover her hair in a modest fashion. Cressa felt the men before she saw them, turning to warn Vasa before she would draw her own weapon.

Vasa was gone. Saiinov was smiling amiably, looking around at the myriad stalls that sold everything from wine to boots to gauzy fabrics that shimmered like magic itself.

"Keep looking ahead," he said, his lips still bent in a cheerful smile.

"But there are — " Cressa began, turning her head to tag the man on the right once again. He'd been closest, a small, nondescript form dressed in shades of forgettable gray and brown. After a brief search, she saw him, his hands busy under a cheap cloak.

Habira appeared behind the unknown follower from the shadow of an awning, her face an impassive mask. She touched him lightly on the neck, and he wobbled like a drunkard, looping off into an alcove where he sat heavily, head lolling. Cressa looked back to where she thought Habira had been walking, only to see Vasa lower her cloak and point a menacing finger at the man on the left, now openly gaping at what only he could see unfolding before him in the crowded street. His face tumbled inward at his defeat, and he melted away into the current of people without a second glance. Some targets were simply too dangerous to approach, no matter what enticements he'd been offered.

That left the man behind them, but Cressa shouldn't have worried. Even as she whirled to see where their last stalker might be, his unconscious form hit the pathway with a solid thump. Saiinov leaned over him, the picture of a caring observer. Cressa watched him frisk the man and secret his findings in a pocket before moving aside to let the crowd rush in, a babble of shouts and whispers as House Windhook moved away without any notice whatsoever.

How had Habira switched cloaks? And positions? Cressa walked along, mute, her mind spinning furiously as she tried to process what she thought happened, but in that instance she was loathe to trust her mind. Vasa's smile made her look like an imp, while Habira remained vigilant but smug. Saiinov was nowhere to be seen, and Cressa realized that he could be anywhere and she wouldn't know.

"They tipped their hand a bit early when we were at the docks, but that's not important now. Saiinov got something from one of them, and that's all we need to find out who sent them. Naturally, my bet goes to the council, although this seems a bit. . ."Vasa searched for a word, until Habira broke in.

"Crude. This is heavy-handed, even for those oafs on the council. I would have expected something a bit less obvious than a triad of lightfingers, no matter how good they were." Habira snorted with derision at the impudence of the council. Cressa sensed that she was more offended by the quality of her opponents than the criminal act, a fact which explained a great deal about why Habira walked through the streets of Sliver as if she owned them. For the moment, the Blightwing chose to keep silent, knowing that she would learn everything in due time. Until then, they strolled, occasionally breaking off to look at the offerings of a merchant. They bought nothing except wine and an assortment of spun glass containers from an apothecary who looked older than Sliver itself.

Before the sun could crest, they were at the end of a curled alley that was clean and well-lit. There was little trash in Sliver, just as there were no beggars or obvious criminals. Everyone in the alley seemed to have a purpose, going to their respective aeries soaring overhead like a forest of bleached bones. The family banners snapped smartly in the breeze, and there were aromas of flowers and spices hanging in the air. Each aerie had wide windows with open shutters, but not at ground level. There were porches and iron railings of delicate designs on every structure, it seemed. Cressa felt the pressure of being watched as she waited, while Saiinov opened the tall double door carved and painted in blue and silver. A massive, scrolling W declared that the aerie belonged to House Windhook. Carved Windbeasts and other more fantastic, lethal-looking creatures curled around the family crest; the implied threat to intruders was clear. *Enter at your own risk.*

They stepped inside to Cressa's gasp. "This is — yours?" Her head swiveled as she took in the rich appointments inside. There was a feeling of wealth in every piece of furniture, from the delicately balanced chairs with their bone armrests, to the subtle colors of the wall hangings depicting House Windhook's members in various pursuits. Cressa recognized a tapestry of Saiinov as a young man, his sword flashing downward in a merciless arc as he beheaded a winged creature that swiped at him with black talons. Its eyes burned a lurid red on the fabric, compelling Cressa to step closer and see if by some miracle the beast was actually alive in the threads, its demonic presence caught for all eternity.

Saiinov stepped alongside her, pulling his gloves off. His expression was thoughtful, rather than a mask of false modesty. "I never wanted mother and father to commission such a thing, but it wasn't my decision." Cressa realized he was embarrassed by the attention, but too mannerly to ask her to ignore the trappings of family history that surrounded them. "We keep this aerie for purposes other than simple pleasure. It's a statement, an investment, if you will.

House Windhook chooses to remain distant, but that doesn't mean that we want the council to think that our location makes us weak. To the contrary, we feel that this place projects power, and thus acts as a form of guarantee that House Windhook will not be caught unaware when the council moves against us."

Cressa's brow furrowed. "But weren't you surprised by my visit?" It seemed that her arrival had been unforeseen, but she was already beginning to doubt her own assessment of every facet that Saiinov and his family presented to her.

He shrugged with an amiability that suggested her question, too, had been expected. She didn't feel offended, though it would have been her right to do so.

"No, the only question was the hour of your arrival."

Habira appeared from behind a tapestry, her boots echoing across the floor like claws on stone. She'd changed into an even more formal jacket and flying pants that clung to her like a second skin. Her expression was neutral, though Cressa could sense the anger simmering just behind her eyes. It was an unsettling sensation, like flying next to a Windbeast that still had a fresh kill on its beak. It was understood that you were not in danger from the monster, but just the same, you wanted distance. It was senseless to tempt fate in that regard.

Habira pulled on supple gloves tooled in the House colors, wriggling her fingers to seat each one. With a nod, she assumed a sunnier disposition. "We knew that a Flyer would arrive at the least, and at the worst, a squad of Sliver enforcers. Neither would have been a surprise." With a curious half-smile, she explained their position. "You dispatched your duties well, Cressa, and we mean you no disrespect. House Windhook knew that this — affair — could only end in confrontation. Rest easy, your errand is nearly complete." Habira turned her attention to Saiinov, addressing her father in a more formal tone, and the air in the room shifted. "Shall we honor our word and present ourselves to be addressed?"

"When your mother is ready. We're going prepared, as I can only assume that Factor Sibilla will be waiting for us when we arrive in The Grievance." Saiinov spat the last word in disgust at the open air chamber where ordinary people were hauled up on false charges, only to see their future evaporate at the whim of a cruel system. Factor Sibilla was notoriously prompt in her arrival for hearings where violence was possible; in fact, she did everything in her considerable power to make certain that blood was shed on the wide, chill floor of The Grievance. There were five Factors in all, but among them only the ancient, chatty Sibilla would present herself before a considerable wait. Even at the peak of power, the council's Factors savored reminding their underlings that their collective strength was greater than almost any force in the known world. It was only one of the petty displays that the Crescent Council thrived upon.

Vasa came out of her dressing chamber, slipping a shimmering cloak over her shoulders. At her hip rode a fine hide bag of indeterminate type; weathered scrolls bulged upward, tied together with a thin ribbon of blue and silver. With a sharp nod, she looked to the door. "We're ready for their opening move."

"We are," Saiinov agreed, his rich voice rolling off the interior spaces like a distant cheer. As they stepped out in the broadway once more, both Saiinov and Habira took a pointed moment to adjust their swords, slung low on the hip for easy access. It wasn't unknown for mishaps to occur on the way to an official inquiry, and the members of House Windhook were unlikely to be taken by surprise.

Cressa cleared her throat and gravely announced that she was placing the entire family in her protective custody from that moment forth. All three of her charges nodded in agreement, walking before her with confident strides as they began to part the crowd, many of whom were whispering and pointing at the family which marched purposefully toward something like war. The long, arcing paths that bordered Sliver all had crossing streets leading to a central plaza. The wide plaza was then ruined with the presence of The Grievance, whose oval malignance rose up from the smooth thoroughfare to dominate the inner sanctum of Sliver. Featureless gray walls were broken only by brutal-looking square entryways; the doors served as access to the interior amphitheater. Glorified rows of benches curved up and away to give the audience maximum access to the spectacle, while denying them the comfort of the resplend-ent chairs from which the council could glare imperiously at anyone in the enormous space. Every detail of The Grievance was designed with two things in mind: that the council should look powerful, and the accused should feel threatened. Until the arrival of House Windhook, the design had largely worked. Saiinov gestured elegantly to his wife and daughter, inviting them ahead of him as they walked in to find the stands nearly filled with buzzing spectators.

It was a rare event. The crowd knew this, and whisp-ers of fascination, anger, and curiosity rose to a hissing rustle as Cressa stepped forward to introduce her charges to the council. The Blightwing raised her hand, palm outstretched and fingers open in the universal gesture asserting her peaceful intentions. She then bowed respectfully toward the sinuous curve of a high table carved from a single Skybeast rib, its surface rubbed to a dull sheen by untold hands. Behind the arrogant façade sat all five Factors; their zeal at seeing House Windhook being muzzled led them to dispense with their tedious displays of power in which they would make one another wait to begin. The air fairly sizzled with excitement at the possible outcomes, and only when Factor Sibilla raised her hand from the middle seat did the audience fall silent. Sibilla's dark, piggish eyes glittered with malicious joy as she swept her ashen hair back from a face that resembled a prune. A smile bared teeth stained by centuries of wind herbs, and her chin warbled with excitement at the prospect of what she might do to the people before her.

Sibilla's eyes flickered over Cressa as she tilted her head in dismissal. There were no thanks, but also no anger. "You people are summoned to answer for the criminal activity in your own house, an issue which has gone on far too long. Where is the boy?" She didn't bother to clarify who she asked for; it was assumed that anyone before the council would be too cowed to respond with anything other than exactly what the Factors wanted to hear.

Sibilla was spectacularly wrong. Saiinov put a hand under his chin and looked thoughtful before turning to Vasa. "Which boy do you think she's asking for? There are so many of them running and flying about like wild beasties, I hardly know where to begin with my answer."

Vasa smiled sweetly, adding a feminine shrug to indicate her helplessness when dealing with such an opaque question. "Could be almost anyone."

"But not I," Habira added helpfully. "You see, mother, I'm a woman. I'm no legal expert, but I think that precludes me from being a part of the answer in this case. In fact, I'd go so far —"

"Enough!" spat Factor Ophaniel. He sat on the far right, a stooped figure of sticklike limbs buried in a voluminous astronomer's robe. The rippling fabric was covered with shifting stars and symbols of arcana, and his hands emerged from the sleeves like pale claws, the knuckles bulbous and pink. He was ancient, and foul, and vainly kept his remaining white hair combed forward like the desperate crowing of an aging rooster. His teeth were long and crooked, and there was spittle at the corners of his mouth. "You were always a slave to your ridiculous pride, Sibilla. Can't you see that these are no outriders being charged with petty defilement? Your tactics are not only worthless, they offend me and waste time." With a dismissive flick of his cadaverous hand, he turned to the man next to him. "Surely you can move this along? I've better things to do than waste my hours on a house filled with miscreants and murderers."

Next to the wizened Ophaniel sat a man unlike any other member of the council. He was in the bloom of early middle age, competent looking, and possessed of a stillness that made him seem more reptilian than angelic. A cloud of inactivity hung about him with the exception of his lips, which quirked with suppressed amusement. His hair was dark, curled, and pulled back from a noble nose and forehead. Factor Castiel's iron-gray eyes were lit from within with a passion for many things, not the least of which was his maniacal love of tradition. To that end, his full lips were pulled to one side in disapproval at the members of House Windhook. They were, in his estimation, a rogue state that had no place in the wider society that Sliver commanded. To see them before him was an opportunity like no other, for unlike three of the five Factors, Castiel was a swordsman of such brilliance that he had yet to be touched in battle. His thick wrist twitched in anticipation as he surveyed Saiinov and Habira; in a slow, insolent arc, he dragged his eyes over them, taking the measure of their bodies and posture. Castiel knew that their poise would reveal more than any statement they might issue while in front of the council.

That was fine by him. Other than Utipa, the youngest and least disciplined Factor, only he understood that after the law had been exhausted, there was only one method that House Windhook could be humiliated.

By the sword.

The second Factor spoke before Castiel could give shape to his thoughts and deliver his litany of planned insults. Nera, a silent, hateful presence on the council, broke her silence with a single question. "Will any of you produce the boy, or shall we move on to the inevitable?"

Silence fell over The Grievance before a storm of whispers could erupt. Even the council had respected the proper forms—until that moment. Nera was largely silent in The Grievance, preferring to let Sibilla do her dirty work, like a trained beast worrying at a juicy bone.

"I think that's abundantly clear, Nera." The relatively young figure on the left spoke, her smile brazen. Factor Utipa was in early adulthood, with olive skin, eyes like midnight, and a streak of deep red in her hair that flared into crimson at the tips. Her eyes sparkled with mischief at the amusement of House Windhook's provocations. She alone could appreciate the will and confidence it took to step into the seat of power and laugh at those holding the reins. "They will not hand the boy over, nor should we expect them to. In a rare case of luck, I tend to agree with Factor Ophaniel, who doubtless wishes to conclude this unpleasant matter before his own death." At the gasps and laughter caroming through The Grievance, Utipa merely smiled, fluttering her lashes at the fossilized members of the council. She studiously avoided eye contact with Castiel, leading the gossips in the audience to begin taking bets as to whether or not she might side with Windhook outright. It wasn't the first time the younger, more vigorous Utipa had broken away from her peers; their simple difference in age was reason enough for her to view the world through less jaundiced eyes.

Ophaniel directed a poisonous look toward the other board members, then tapped a bony finger onto the table in anger. "I care nothing for the barbs of an upstart, nor do I regard House Windhook as anything short of criminal. If they choose to flaunt the legitimate rule of the council, then a price will be paid." He drew in a rattling breath as a skeletal smile parted his lips. "And that price will be high."

"We are aware of the law, council members." Vasa's retort was calm, her voice even. There was only resignation in her mention of a legal system so arcane that it kept every resident of Sliver and beyond in a constant state of upheaval. For the Crescent Council, fear and blood were good for business.

"Oh you are?" Sibilla huffed, her eyes flashing with hate. "What a fascinating admission, given that to this moment you and your so-called house has done nothing but show wanton disregard for the authority of Sliver and this council. You claim to know the law, but ignore it. That makes you a criminal, in my opinion."

Nera pointed at Saiinov, who regarded her blandly. "We could accept—not like, but accept this behavior if you were ignorant savages from some untamed range in the east, but no, you and your vicious brood are fully versed in the legal commands we issue here. The law is ageless, and you are not. You will see this first hand, Windhook, and I for one am thrilled to be a part of this day." Her eyes fluttered in momentary pleasure, giving her the appearance of a saint in ecstasy. "Do you understand what happens next, Windhook? Do you grasp that your family will live and die in this chamber, no matter what petty grievances you might have?" Her lips were drawn back in a hideous approximation of a smile. Habira took note of her long teeth and feral look, but said nothing. Let the old ones think that ancient tradition alone could cage the family who would bring Sliver to a standstill.

"What, then?" Vasa asked, hands on hips. Her smooth transition from legal scholar to insolent enemy was seamless. Factor Utipa suppressed a smirk at the woman, whose aggressive posture set the council's anger surging yet again.

This time, it was Castiel who responded, his voice a silken threat. "You'll be given three opportunities to rebuff the decree of this council." He looked around presumptively at the other Factors, awarding the barest of glances. "I speak for the entire council when I say even *that* opportunity is beyond generous. Whether you survive the tests or not is irrelevant; but consider yourselves honored to be given the chance to die fighting for your traitorous, heretical cause."

A rolling wave of laughter and shock burst forth from

the stands as everyone in attendance knew what the outcome would be. Death, and in a spectacular manner. The Factors were not selected for their incompetence, despite their great age. They fought and schemed their way to the top, meaning that anyone on the council was a past master of their chosen art. Even the fossil Ophaniel could kill with the flick of his fingers; his grasp of the arcane arts had been legendary more than a century earlier.

That left the question of Utipa. She'd grown to power as a commander among Skywatchers, her martial skills surpassed only by her odd likeability even as she wielded power within The Grievance and Sliver. She was aloof, and even friendly at times, but on occasion she would lash out to remind everyone that she was anything but a pushover. Her genius was the ability to be consistently under-estimated. Every rival she'd dispatched on her rise to the top had said the same thing: they never saw it coming. As a fair judge, she was often seen as the lone ray of light for anyone standing before the council, but at that moment her face was inscrutable. Whatever her thoughts were about House Windhook, she wasn't ready to tip her hand. Yet.

Saiinov gestured toward Utipa, his manner graceful and touched with an air of respect. It was the first such concession on his part, and it angered the other four Factors even as it pleased Utipa. "Factor Utipa, a point for consideration, if I may?"

"You may." She inclined her head less than an inch, but it was enough. Ophaniel grew purple with repressed anger, while Castiel looked as if he might vault the table and draw steel on the entire family. Nera and Sibilla sat mute, watching the moment unfold to see if there was an advantage they could gain.

"House Windhook accepts Factor Castiel's reasonable suggestion that we place our faith in three distinct tests, but I — excuse me, *we*" — he glanced at Vasa, who smiled knowingly — "ask that the tests be set at this moment."

The crowd noise doubled until Castiel raised a hand of warning, settling the uprising to a tolerable bustle. "You make no demands of this council, Windhook. You are subjects, not partners." His oily smile radiated malice, but it slid from Saiinov without sticking.

"Naturally, I only wished to express my desire that the third and final test be a duel between Factor Castiel and myself, and that it be done with unadorned longswords, while bound within the rules of the fighting circle." Now the crowd exploded, but Saiinov waved them to silence with a jocular smile. "Please, please, friends. There is one more detail to impart."

Crowds have a sense for when something shocking is about to occur, and the stands of angels in The Grievance were no different. They cocked their heads as one, looking at the house leader radiating confidence, his legs apart and chin thrust up to regard the Factors with something like tolerant curiosity.

After a moment that stretched into disrespect, Nera's patience finally cracked. "Well? What idiocy do you wish to spout now?" Her words were bitter and jagged, her face like a closed fist.

"Before I make my request, I offer my daughter Habira as contestant against Factor Utipa, and my wife Vasa asks that she be allowed to match skills with Factor Ophaniel." In the new uproar, Saiinov casually added, "Oh, and with the utmost respect for this august council, I would like it clear that my match against Factor Castiel will be to the death."

Without another word, House Windhook turned on their collective heel and left to the roar of angels who knew change was in the air.

Cressa led the family through a crowd that stared at Saiinov, openmouthed with awe and more than a little fear. Among angels, the council feared no one, but an unknown trio from a rogue house had challenged the Crescent Council in its own space. It was unheard of, and thus, the event made House Windhook into a threat that was immediate and contagious. Angels were rigidly structured despite the chaos that surrounded Sliver, so it came as no surprise that the trip to their aerie was free of any interference for the family that dared to fight back.

Once inside, Cressa fought a moment of disconnection, wondering if her spirit was leaving her body. She shook her wings lightly before leaning against a wall where paintings climbed skyward in an offset pattern. Her heart raced and she nearly jumped when Habira handed her a flute of wine, so cold that it seemed to sear her fingers.

"What do you see? Up there?" Saiinov pointed at the paintings, a patient look on his face. His voice was that of a teacher using gentle inquiry to find out what his pupil might know.

After a long look, Cressa shook her head. It was too much — the family, their bravado, and even the wine on her tongue, bright and cold. "I don't know. I see — us."

He nodded with approval before turning away to pour more wine for Vasa. "That's true. And that doesn't concern you?" Handing his wife her fluted glass, he squared on Cressa, his manner expectant, but not unkind.

"Should it?" Her confusion grew. Each painting was a past glory of House Windhook, or the families from which they came. There were scenes of victory, and sadness, and themes varying in color and clarity, but always, always about war. "They're all violent. Every one of them."

Saiinov's smile was paternal and sad. "Indeed. We are a people who thrive on conflict, but we weren't always as such. Do you know that there was a time we were regarded as harbingers of good? That we, as a people, were the messengers of joy and light?" Disgust passed over his handsome face, turning it into a condemnation of every-thing around them. "And now? Look at us. We squabble and brawl like children for control of lands that no one cares for, save to place their name on them. There are warlords in the far west, and rogue armies to the south. Did you know that?"

Cressa was genuinely stunned. She was too young to remember the War of the Compass, and too invisible to be told about it. "No, I thought the council ruled. Everywhere."

Vasa laughed, but gently. "They do not even control their own lands, Flyer. If they did, why would we be here, plotting their demise?" At Cressa's gasp, she explained. "Long ago, my husband and I made the decision to become parents, but with conditions. We would not allow our children to become fodder for a system that used them as disposable warriors in an endless war, not when each of them had the potential for greatness. So, we began to design our own future, and in that vision there is no grasping hand of the Crescent Council."

"Bu—but they've ruled forever!" Cressa nearly shouted. Her skin grew cold at the mechanical tone Vasa used when she began discussing the end of the world as she knew it.

"Not true, and no longer. We will challenge them, defeat them, and set our people on the path back to peace. We've waited our whole lives for this opportunity, and it has taken considerable luck along with our years of work to come this close. So I ask you, Cressa the Blightwing, if you are willing to be on our side of this conflict, because rest assured, we are most certainly going to war." Vasa watched her carefully, marking the rise and fall of her chest as she worked through the weight of what might be.

The choices were clear, and neither seemed logical, let alone possible. She could spend her life as a servant of the council, living as a shadow on the fringe of the world, or she could dare to ascend with a family who sought nothing short of an empire. They didn't *seem* power-mad or unstable, at least not to her, but she was a child next to them. She knew precious little of the world, and even fewer facts about the history of her own people. She began to pace in silence as the shadows changed position across the upper reaches of the aerie. Dusk approached, and the weight of a decision began to loom just as the night forced its way across the cirrus clouds visible through the high windows above them.

Even when she was young, Cressa had always been keenly aware of her own instincts. She felt and listened to herself, even when others would not. Cressa was, above all else, a practical being who understood that there were rarely more than two choices in any given situation. She would side with Windhook, and possibly die, or she would live out her days in a cold approximation of life.

Cressa settled her wings before looking directly at Vasa, whose face was unreadable save an expectancy around her eyes. She fingered the long feathers at the end of her left wing, their color a uniform tone of shame. "What do you need from me?"

Vasa didn't even smile. Instead, she began to speak, and the world fell away as Cressa listened to the plan that would bring endless war or perfect peace to the only place she had ever known.

CHAPTER THIRTEEN:

Thursday

You're joking, right?" Livvy's breath caught in her throat. Keiron wasn't smiling, and if she had to go through one more second of being played for a fool —

"Not a prince." He patted the air with his hands, but his face remained a solemn wall. "I'm not a prince, nor will I ever be one, and while we're at it, I've never even met one."

"Okay," Livvy drawled, her senses still on high alert for disappointment. After the first real kiss of her life, she wasn't ready for a lie. "Do I have to invite you to explain, or is this something you're going to do because you can sense my desire to kick you?"

"I'll explain, of course, but maybe down by the river? I'd like to catch the end of the sun?" His tone was part plea and part apology. With a regal tilt of her head, Livvy let him take her arm, and they began a slow walk toward the library doors. Dozer gave them both a conspiratorial wink as they passed by, and if the regulars took notice of them it was only to glance up from their books. They were, to most of the world, invisible. It gave Livvy a sensation of intimacy she'd never known before, and she let the feeling wrap itself around her, savoring each second as they made their way outside into the unusually bitter air.

"When did it get cold again?" Livvy shivered, leaning into Keiron's side without thought.

He put an arm around her as they stepped delicately over the rain-slicked path; there were chill puddles everywhere and the taste of snow in the wind.

"I thought this was supposed to be spring."

"It was. Where are the ducks?" He looked at the grim river hurrying past in a steel gray ribbon. The friendly channel of a day earlier was gone, replaced by a cold, charmless expanse of water flecked with foam and the occasional log.

"They're not here. I thought they were full time beggars." She craned her neck to look, but Livvy saw nothing, save Frank and his hot dog cart some distance away. She shuddered at the memory of her failed lunch, taking another look at the trees that grew in evenly spaced squares along the Riverwalk. Even the small buds on their limbs seemed withdrawn in the face of a frigid wind, and the wide bank of angry clouds was only moving closer. "I think those might bring some nasty stuff. We probably shouldn't stay for long, and I have to be back in a while, anyway." She pointed at the looming bank, growing closer by the minute.

"Okay, let's walk slowly and turn back. I'll talk on the way. Deal?"

"Deal. Okay, go. Tell me everything wild and wonderful about yourself and the mysterious lands from that book." She twined her fingers through his, but gently. Even that gesture was new to her, and she didn't want to presume. She also wanted to enjoy it.

"I'm almost certain that my family history runs through that book, but I'm not sure how. I remember my mother telling me some vague stories about how and why that place matters, but to be honest, most of the memories I have aren't good, at least not about wherever the council lived." He started to go on, but Livvy held up their hands, fingers till joined together lightly.

"Sorry to interrupt, but this is going to bother me if I don't mention it." Livvy stopped and turned him to her so that their eyes met directly. The wind picked up his hair and made it into a living thing, framing his surprise in a dark halo of curls that moved of their own volition.

"Mention what?" His response was slow, careful. Like Livvy had been for most of her life.

She looked at their hands again. "Is this a date? I mean, a real date?" Her voice was even and strong. She was curious, but not hostile.

"I guess it is. I mean, we kissed, and we're walking next to a body of water. I think that qualifies. Why?" He smiled, and there was caution there, still.

"Because I'm worth it." In those four words, she left the bitterness of her previous lessons behind while standing her ground as she edged closer to being someone else. Perhaps an adult, although most of her life had been filled with concerns no child would ever endure. Her soul might be young, but her body was older, though the shared kiss made her feel light, even giddy. It had been goodness distilled in the touch of their lips.

He didn't laugh, or run, or mock her. He pulled her hand to his lips and kissed it, then the rest of her joined him. Speaking into her hair, she heard him say, "Yes, you are." They stood that way for a while until the first drops of frigid rain began to fall. Only then did they separate from their embrace to begin their walk with new, quicker steps.

"Okay, as long as that's clear." She smiled up at him, feeling a raw kind of energy that she knew must be confidence, and it was welcome.

"I can already tell that this date is the best of your life." Keiron looked at her slyly until she narrowed her eyes. "You stopped counting your steps. I'd say that's a good sign, right?"

It was true. She hadn't counted since they left the stairs descending to the Riverwalk, and yet her lungs were filled with the cold, sweet air of the day. "I have better things to do right now, and stop changing the subject."

"You're the one who asked for a dating status clarification; right in the middle of an oncoming storm, I might add. I'm the victim here." When she rolled her eyes, he conceded the point and moved on, but his arm went around her just a bit tighter. The wind was picking up, and they had to go up two flights of stairs. "While we go up, I'll start telling you what I know. The condensed version." They began the slow climb. "I know where I'm from, but I don't know why it's important. I know that the country was more or less in a state of constant war, and that my family made it out or something, but I'm not sure how. My mom and dad talked about their parents, and grandparents, and all of them seemed to hate the people on the Crescent Council because they treated people like things instead of, well, people. You know, like toys, or servants." They made it to the landing of the first flight as the breeze began spitting snow. It was grainy and sharp, and it stung.

Livvy nodded, out of breath but in good spirits. She rolled her hand forward twice, telling him that they could go on. She would save her breath for the top, when they got there. It wasn't far away, and Keiron was strong.

He took up his explanation as they ascended. "I look like my dad, but I think like my mom. At least that's what they've told me. What about you?" His question surprised her as they took the last step. Snowflakes were beginning to swirl around them now, and Keiron never relented in his support. He kept them moving steadily toward the library doors even as she considered an answer.

"What about . . . what?" It was half of a gasp, but better than she'd expected.

"Your mom and dad. Who do you look like?" He pulled the door open with one arm as a welcome rush of warmer air struck them. It seemed nearly tropical compared to what they left behind a few feet away.

Livvy took a moment, just breathing and looking around. It felt good to use an old trick to gain her wind, but then she had to deal with the facts of her answer. "Neither. I'm adopted." Before Keiron could protest, she reassured him that her feelings weren't hurt with a tug at his arm. "Don't. They love me, and I love them more than anything. They took a sick baby with half a heart and made me into their daughter. I don't just love my parents, I respect them, too. They both work at a local college. Dad teaches chemistry and mom teaches languages. I guess you could say that they're both very gentle people." Her smile was unabashed at the thought of them walking out the door together each morning as they went to the campus. Livvy's house was only three blocks away from the small college, and if the weather was nice her parents walked to work, hand in hand. Nothing seemed to rattle them. Ever. She'd been present at more bad news from doctors than almost anyone else in the world, but her mom and dad would just stand firm in the face of each new decree that meant another surgery, or another test. Honestly, the pain was something she could live with, but their support made it a distant thing, like an irritating voice calling to her from an unknown distance.

"Oh, hey, Wheezer. See you've got someone to carry you around like a pet." Ashley stood in front of Britney and Jessica, a sour grin on her pretty face. Neither of the other girls looked up from their phones; they couldn't even be bothered to acknowledge Livvy. She figured that was progress, of a sort. If they were looking down with their mouths closed, then she could deal with Ashley.

Livvy looked down at her hand, still twined with Keiron's. When she made eye contact with Ashley, the biting retort died on her tongue. Here was a girl who had unevenly drawn eyebrows and anger painted over the rest of what should have been a beautiful face. At that moment, she didn't feel anything for Ashley except pity. She spoke calmly, her words even and merciful, although Ashley could never have taken them that way. "I'm sorry that you don't know what this feels like."

Ashley flinched as if struck, which, in a way, she had been. Before she could throw any more of her poisonous words into the air, Keiron pushed past the three girls, Livvy in tow. The silence was heavy and a little bit sad, but then Livvy wasn't going to let the feeling she had be swept away in the face of petty cruelty. Keiron let go of her hand as they came to a rest like migrating birds, their feet in front of Dozer, who looked on approvingly like a mother hen.

"Glad you kids are back," he chided, but there was a laugh waiting somewhere in his greeting. "You've got about thirty seconds to get over here before someone notices you were gone a tiny bit longer than your, ahh, *scheduled* break." He looked pointedly at her chair, causing Livvy's face to transform into a look of mournful acceptance. "She can see you tomorrow, Keiron, but only if you swear to have her back on time?" Dozer adopted the look of a big brother returning home from college to find his sister on the front porch with her date, their faces a mask of shared conspiracy. He lifted a brow at Keiron, who dipped his head with a severity that made him look much older.

"I wouldn't dream of anything else. I understand that there are rules, Dozer. After all, this is a library." He leaned across the desk and kissed Livvy quickly and decisively, their lips meeting for a charged second that caused her to blush crimson. "Until tomorrow."

At the door, he turned and waved before going down the stairs, his long form disappearing out into the growing gloom as the day surrendered to dusk. In a swirl of flakes, she saw him open the door on the first floor, wave once more, and vanish.

"A question for you, dear." Dozer spun in his chair, settling in to debrief Livvy with a practiced air. "Up until the moment that guy walked in here, what would you have said was your favorite part of this library?" His eyes twinkled with unchecked delight at how her day was progressing. He was a true friend; it was obvious on his face that he was enjoying seeing her live a little.

She didn't hesitate. "The smell of the books."

Dozer laughed at her instant reply, then put his hands on the desk and tilted his head at an angle of disbelief. "Oh. You're serious?" He was dubious, but his smile came back in a flash. "The smell?"

Livvy nodded, looking off into the expanse of shelves. Books had been a companion of hers when the only other thing in her life had been pain or uncertainty; sometimes both. They kept her company during long nights sitting up, feeling as if she were drowning in an ocean that only she could see, but turning a page in a book was always enough to keep her steady. To keep her from crying, or screaming. Sometimes, she thought books had been the only thing other than the love of her parents that kept her from quitting. They were old friends who never left, and always took her by the hand to go someplace her broken body could not. All of these thoughts swirled in her mind like the growing snow outside, but she chose to keep most of them to herself. Even Livvy had a room in her mind that was hers alone, and not to be shared with the world outside. So, she drew a breath and explained, while Dozer looked on, his eyes soft with understanding.

"Sometimes, I can stand in one of the reference rows, or the sections where books pile up dust because no one wants to read them. The air is more still there, you know, and the smell of all that old paper, so filled with stories — it piles up like the scent of a summer storm that's coming over the horizon. You know the kind? Like where the wind picks up, and there's something so totally unique that you can't think of anything else except the rain that's on the way? That's how the books smell to me, but it isn't rain. It's age, and wisdom, and even a little bit of sadness when I think about the stories going unread. There's no other smell in the world like it, and opening a book just intensifies the whole thing. To me, there are only two things in the world that smell like home. One is my mother's perfume, and the other is the scent of my father's study. It's crammed with such beautiful old books, and it always smells like the room was waiting for me to get there." Tears filled her eyes at the memory of it all, although she wasn't sure why since her parents and all of that life were close by, and just fine. In that moment, it all seemed incredibly distant, but maybe it was the snow outside.

Maybe, if she was honest, it was partially from watching Keiron walk out into the gray of a cold, snowy dusk. Their time together had been more than a simple talk; Livvy felt like something was building. She wasn't stupid, nor was she lonely. But the feel of his hand in hers was like the curtain being pulled back on a life that had eluded her.

Up until now.

"I'm sorry, Liv." Dozer's words were so soft she might have imagined them. He was leaning to her, his hands taking hers so kindly that she could do nothing but watch as he put her palms together, his own fingers covering hers. "I wish you'd never been through — I don't know, all of it." He shrugged, defeated by the terrible beauty of her life before the library. It was a motion of such generosity that she felt a tear slide down her cheek before it fell to the desk with a soft patter. It was a noise of admission; her pain made real, only to be turned back by this kind boy who called her friend. He swept the tear away like an errant spark, preventing a fire that could only have hurt her in the place she needed protection the most. Her heart.

CHAPTER FOURTEEN:

Aerie

ressa listened. She heard plans of such a scale she felt like an insect sitting before a Windbeast, watching the massive creature's feet in order to run toward safety. The people of House Windhook did not think like her, nor did they shy away from ideas that some would call justice but others might call treason. Grandiose was, to them, another word for ambition, and they regarded their aims as necessary rather than a mere play for power. After a time, Habira and Saiinov vanished into a large room, closing the doors behind them as they chattered in high spirits about weapons and war. In moments, the brassy ringing of swordplay drifted into the main room where Vasa held court with the messenger who was learning that the council was not as immortal as it seemed.

In fact, as the lady detailed the intentions of House Windhook, it occurred to Cressa that there had to be a reason why these things were being revealed to her, of all people. True, she had no love for the council, but one word from her could bring the might of the guard crashing into the aerie, and no amount of bravery would stop them from trussing Saiinov and his family up without ceremony.

That left one possibility. Vasa *wanted* the council to know. At an appropriate gap in the conversation, Cressa interrupted, a look of modest apology acting as a buffer against any unintended offense. "Lady, as much as I appreciate your confidence in me, why are you telling me this? What you describe is punishable by death. Why me? Why now, or at all, given what you seem to be intent on creating here in the Sliver?"

Vasa lifted a sculpted brow. "Oh? And what is that?"

Cressa sputtered, but drew a calming breath to lend clarity to her thoughts. "Chaos. You're bringing chaos to this place, and you seem to have been planning it for a long time. Why?"

A triumphant shout from Saiinov announced some martial victory in the sparring that went on, unabated. When the voices quieted once more, Vasa pointed to a carved bookshelf along the near wall. "That book bound in silver and blue. Look at it." She made a shooing gesture to Cressa, but not without smiling.

Cressa reached out and up then lifted the tall, wide book from its place of honor in between other less richly appointed volumes. Scanning the spine, she nodded appreciatively. "It's your history, or more specifically, House Windhook. What of it, lady? Don't all families have such things?"

"Did yours?" Vasa stood, coming over to the shelf with quick, decisive steps. Even at an increased pace, there was a liquidity to her steps that Cressa found magical. "My apology. That sounded bitter; I meant nothing of the sort. I merely wished to point out that not all families have their histories in a written form, and there is good reason."

"Why? All it takes is some hide, and parchment, and ink. Any family can afford that." It was true. There was little cost in writing, let alone something as meaningful as a family's story. If anything, that kind of effort would take precedent over other more glamorous pursuits. To the people from Cressa's world, where they came from was as important as where they were going. History was a confirmation of one's worth, and if necessary could always be altered to fit a different opinion of exactly who or what house mattered most.

"True, but a better point might be to consider what the history is concerned with. There are victories and losses. Birth, death, love. Even crime can be found, if it adds to the tale for some families."

Cressa snorted at that, but otherwise held her tongue.

Vasa walked back to her seat, taking measured steps as her thoughts deepened. When she settled and turned to Cressa, her eyes were narrowed as she considered what to say next. "In the few conversations we've had, do you know what surprises me most about you?"

Cressa started at that. It was a hard turn away from their previous topic, and she felt as if unsteady currents were under her wings. The sensation was unsettling, as Vasa seemed able to change course without warning, leaving Cressa wondering once again as to the lady's true intent. "No, lady. And I can't begin to guess." She fell quiet, waiting. The clash of steel echoed through the aerie again. It had a rhythm to it completely unlike war, and to Cressa's limited experiences, sounded more like dancing.

"You never asked us if Garrick did it." Vasa's words were statement, not question, and delivered with the certainty of a woman who was co-ruler of a house that verged on open warfare with an empire. Never before had Cressa heard such power delivered in a casual manner.

Seconds trickled away without a sound, until Cressa realized she'd stopped breathing. Vasa sat with a placid expression, waiting, her eyes pinning the young woman with a look of such frank curiosity that it verged into rudeness. Shadows moved across the upper windows; it could have been any number of flying things interrupting the brilliance of the afternoon sun, but the flicker was so fast as to be instantaneous. When it became apparent that Vasa was content to wait until moonrise for an answer, the Flyer was left with no choice but to answer with a question of her own.

"Why did you *make* him do it?" Cressa asked, her voice so loaded with curiosity she felt herself lean forward slightly as the question departed her like a fleeing spirit. It had nagged her for some time as she'd listened to the lady speaking of plans and actions and minutiae that gradually convinced her nothing these people did was unintended. Nothing was accidental, or lucky, or even open to interpretation. They weren't cold, just thorough, and that led her to the conclusion that Garrick's crime had been nothing more than the completion of a web so dense that to pluck one string meant you would be tangled in all of them, a condition that could be fatal if the spiders of House Windhook decided you were prey rather than friend. Where the council was an implacable wall of power, Vasa's plans felt more like a storm arriving after having built on the horizon for days. It was no less dangerous, but more unknown, and therefore a thing to be avoided.

Cressa knew that time had passed. The only thing to

be done was ride out the winds in the best manner she knew, which was a dangerous decision in its own right. For her, the decision of a lifetime was at hand.

She had to pick a side. Based on her limited knowledge of both parties, she would be entering into a fray that was nothing short of civil war. On one wing, there was her status—a nobody or worse in a society that lived on position and appearance. On the other wing, there was the issue of trust. How could she side with a family who had, in a few short hours, shown her that their capacity for cunning surpassed even the most warlike families of Sliver and beyond? It was a leap of faith unlike anything she'd ever known, and the only remaining question hinged on how Lady Vasa chose to answer Cressa's impertinent demand about Garrick. Cressa let her wings rustle in agitation before she stilled herself with an effort. It wouldn't do to advertise her uncertainty, even if it was obvious to anyone who looked at her body language. She was on the edge and wanting an answer.

Vasa pierced her with a pair of eyes that were nearly hypnotic from the intellect behind them. "Garrick didn't really have a choice. He's a vain boy, but not without his qualities, and before you ask me, yes. I love him, from wingtip to wingtip in spite of his many flaws. That's part of being a parent, and it's a burden that Saiinov and I are only too willing to bear." She stood and began pacing, before making her way to a tall table where a bottle and glasses rested. After pouring two flutes, she handed one to Cressa before walking away, her thoughts building like an oncoming wind. Cressa sipped out of courtesy; the wine was light and airy, nearly transparent.

"Do you know what we do, and have done for all our

adult lives? Saiinov, me, Habira?"

"I know your titles. I know that Habira is a fighter, any fool could see that. As to the rest of you, I'm not really sure I believe what you say, at least in terms of your chosen occupations. I think there's a lot more to you than you admit, and you're going to explain it all to me right now because you sense that I need to choose a direction." Cressa regarded the Lady with an even look, showing that she wasn't going to be ignored. Not now, and certainly not in the face of a conflict that would likely be unavoidable. The skies were going to be dangerous, and soon. *More dangerous*, she corrected herself.

"Ahh, you're observant, and you can see in the distance. That's good." Vasa leaned against the wine table, one hand lazily running along the carved edge. "We are a people of war, but manners, too. We love to pretend that our veneer of civilization is permanent, but that is merely one of the lies that we tell ourselves. Does that make you sad? To know that the people who condemned you as a killer are no better?" Vasa watched carefully as Cressa gave the question some thought.

The Lady had something like approval on her fine features, content to wait for an actual answer rather than a meaningless response. "I never thought that anyone was my better. Or worse. I didn't really think about other people at all." It was bleak, but honest.

Vasa nodded gravely at that. "You've struck close to the truth, although I doubt the council members would admit having such a tendency toward animal behavior. What do you think I do during all of my days in the confines of my spaces?"

"You are a scholar. I guess that means you read? And

write?" She shrugged slightly to indicate her lack of a clear idea.

"That's a start, certainly, but I really only do one thing." Vasa held out her hands as if holding an invisible thread in each, then began to weave them together in the same motion one might use to braid a child's hair. "My family were saving people, as are all of the families with scholars among them. So, I take history" — she bobbed one hand lightly — "and sorcery, and I twist them together to make something different. Much as an armorer might take humble things to make a chest piece of radiant beauty, I take things that, on their own, are not impressive at all. Sorcery is common, even tedious. Ahh, but when paired with something from the past or future, then it becomes an entirely different force. It is, in a sense, the strength of a beating heart. Life itself. Do you see?"

"No, I — the future?"

Vasa raised a finger, nodding. "A critical distinction. Before I go on, let me ask you. Do you know who you are? Not Cressa, the Blightwing, but who you are as a being."

"I'm a person." Her tone revealed she was tiring of guessing games, leading Vasa to pat the air gently in assurance that there was something to be gained from their conversation, but all in good time.

"You are. And so am I, but to the beings beneath us, we are not human. None of this" — she waved a hand around at the magnificence of Sliver — "is real to them. They think of us as heavenly bodies, fighting for justice or flitting from cloud to cloud on wings of spun gold. They know nothing of who we are, or where we've come from, and that's why my work is so critical. It's also why we can't allow the council to continue their ruin of our skies." Vasa spoke as if the council was falling ashes. It was chilling to hear.

"If we—I mean, if they are not us, then what? And why can you see into the future? You still haven't answered my question about that." She wasn't letting Vasa dodge her, not now.

"When Garrick pushed his brother, he knew that there was more to it than a long fall. It was a journey, a piercing of the sky to go somewhere else, and some*when* else. He did it because I found something in my research years ago. It was a single page from a book, but I like to think of it as a distant mirror. On one side, there is us. On the other . . . is the past." Vasa looked down, her eyes bright with the light of discovery. She seemed nearly fevered, but still in control. "Yes, I said the past. My son Keiron has gone through the light of days to find and save a girl who will help us win this war. And he did it because I asked him to. So did his father." At Cressa's gasp, she smiled. "You have no idea the tears I shed when it became obvious that we had to send him back, back to find a girl with a heart made for battle. There is only one reason in the universe that I would willingly send my son through a tear in the sky, back to a world that might not even be real for us."

"Why?" Cressa's voice shook. She was listening to a mother describe the sacrifice of her child to a realm that might only be shadows. It was evil. Incomprehensible. For a child like Cressa, it was like reliving a death in the family, standing there next to Vasa's serene acceptance of something so ghastly.

It was inhuman.

Vasa took her hands, and Cressa was so numb she didn't pull away. "When I told you I worked in both the past and the future, I meant exactly that. I look into the past for truths, and occasionally I find something useful. But it is here, in the now, that most of my work takes place. It is the modern documents that have the most power —which I can braid into sorcery of such a scope that the council cannot begin to imagine what we may do to them."

"You find these things here? Now? But I thought you said—"

"We *are* the people below, or rather, we were. We *are* their future—what they become, if given a chance, and without that girl, we are doomed. I sent my son into the past because I know it had already happened, and without him there is no us. No today. And, although it's murky, without Keiron's journey, there is certainly no future."

An exultant Saiinov approached, his face glistening with sweat over a look of mild gloating. "She's ready." He flexed his shoulders experimentally before adding, "I don't know if I am, but our daughter is beyond prepared." Taking note of Cressa's stricken look, he wiped his face with a cloth and took stock of the counter space. With a nod to himself, he held out an arm. "Join me, Flyer? I need to walk the Merchant's Twist, and it would be improper to do so without you guarding me."

Cressa stood, numb. She'd just learned her own past lay beneath her feet, and any future she had was sifting through her fingers like the mist of an early morning fog. In one revelation, Vasa told her more than she'd ever wanted to know, and yet here she was, expected to act as if it were even possible for her to guard Saiinov, let alone make him obey. She rose on unsteady feet, thankful for the muscular presence of his arm, and as they departed she heard nothing of what was said. It was as if she'd left her own body behind only to watch her thoughts uncoil, one merciless truth at a time.

Cressa cleared her throat, but it failed to shake her free of the previous moments. "What do you need?" Her voice was a quaking croak.

"It isn't what I need, Cressa, although some more wine and oilcloth would be welcome. One can never have too much of either. One takes care of your spirits, the other protects your blades. Neither are things that can be neglected; at least not if you plan on surviving this den of serpents." Saiinov was in a fine mood, amiable and relaxed. The combat between him and his daughter unleashed a kind of peace about the man, softening his edges into something less menacing. For the first time, Cressa saw him as a person rather than the physical embodiment of House Windhook's martial abilities. It was much more to her liking, and by the time they were away from the street where the aerie was tucked, her nerves returned to something more like normalcy. He gestured grandly at the Twist, which opened before them in a raucous blast of noise and color. "Have you ever spent any time here? It's quite a lesson."

"No, I'm usually waiting for an assignment, and we never visited when I was young." She craned her head, then stopped, thinking it best not to look like a visitor in from the outer reaches.

"No, go ahead, look around. We'll not be harassed, I assure you." He was right, people moved subtly aside to make room for Saiinov, even going so far as to dip their wings in acknowledgment of his passing. The vendors took on a softer, more respectful tone with him as well. There was no yelling, only the occasional hearty greeting as one voice or another rose up to bring attention to their wares. The street was more crowded than anything Cressa had seen in her life; it was impossible to move without brushing wings with people hurrying, or strolling, or even standing in deep conversation with a crafter over something that they could not live without. There were stalls with curing hides, acrid in the air, their colors brilliant from new dyes and bone eyelets gleaming in the sunlight. She saw bottles of every shape and size holding liquids that were wine, or wind herbs, or perhaps both. Some were filled with mist, some with sand — a rarity, she knew, and others still were laden with substances for which she had no words.

Saiinov seemed to know *everyone*, but he eventually made his way to a venerable older man who had a simple stall in which he sold cloths imbued with everything needed to protect a fine blade. The smell clinging to him was pleasant, like a blend of sunlight and oils. After a negotiation in which she remained silent out of respect for the process, Saiinov purchased four distinct lengths of hide, or cloth — she couldn't be sure what the actual material was, but each was rolled tightly upon itself, edges tucked in to form a neat packet with a loop for carrying.

"What are those?" Her expression was one of frank curiosity. She was recovering some of her natural vigor.

"Each cloth is used to restore an edged weapon when there isn't time for a whetstone. They're magical in nature, but originally they were just thin hides with grease and grit. Now, the same effect is achieved with something more elegant." He nodded at the swinging bundles. "We'll need wine and some other basic items for The Grievance, since it would be sheer foolishness to expect the council to treat us like guests. No, we'll be handled roughly, I think."

"As if trials by combat aren't rough treatment?" She was only partially joking.

He stopped, letting the crowd stream around them like a flock of birds. "I'm an experienced fighter, and my wife is — well, she's nothing that the council has ever seen before. They're all old and cagey, but Vasa is something beyond their experience."

"I notice you didn't mention your daughter in that sentence."

"I did not, and that's because she's the great unknown in this plan. Habira is fierce and quick, but she's also young." He looked up into the sun. It was lower, but still brilliant. What he hoped to find in the slanting rays, Cressa didn't know, but there seemed to be a search happening before her. She found it unsettling. For a moment, the hard edges returned to Saiinov's face, but it might have been the hour of the day.

"Can she lose?" The question was like the pealing of a distant bell that couldn't be ignored. It hung between them before he smiled, and once again Saiinov looked younger.

"Anyone can lose, but yes. She can. Will she?" He shook his head, and there was a solidity to the gesture that made Cressa believe it. "I won't let it happen, nor will her mother. As far as the council is concerned, they're hardly used to fighting fair."

"You mean they would actually break protocol in combat? Isn't that grounds for — "

"Rebellion?" His taunt landed home, and she winced. He'd led her into stating the one thing that she found difficult to accept, but stripped bare in his logic it seemed to be the only way that House Windhook could survive.

They had to win, and that meant she needed them to

emerge victorious, no matter what the cost. They couldn't just defeat the three Factors in their chosen fields, they had to do so in a way that left Sliver convinced of their right to revolt. Around them, the business day was closing as the glows of lamps began to cast shadows, cutting into the weak sun arrowing down between aeries and other buildings. Cressa considered her position and what it meant, and realized that for several minutes Saiinov hadn't spoken.

"What is it?" She looked at him in mild alarm, wondering why he'd gone quiet, but his expression was hardly one of fright. If anything, he seemed to be taking the measure of everything around them.

"I wonder if this will still exist tomorrow night." He grinned and began walking back to the aerie, his wings folded in contentment at they stood on the brink of revolution.

CHAPTER FIFTEEN:

Friday

*J*t looks kind of regal." Livvy held the blue and silver book delicately, despite its unwieldy heft. She was in the process of learning the majestic history of a place that frankly sounded like a rather fancy brawl. There were shifting alliances, angry councils, and people whose sole purpose seemed to be making grandiose speeches during which they would point skyward and shout, as if by sheer volume they could overwhelm their opponents. It all sounded rather medieval, and after a few pages she gratefully closed the cover with a muffled thump.

"What *are* you reading? Some sort of auto repair manual? And why?" Dozer looked at the book as if it was a scorpion poised to strike. His own tastes ran to volumes he could read in a day without breaking his conversation with Livvy. He had literary standards, and they were intentionally mediocre, unlike his hair.

"If you must know, it's a history of House Windhook. I'm sure you've heard of it, being so worldly and all." She attempted to sneer, but he waved her off with a look of pity.

"Please. I'm telling you this from the heart. Leave the snark to me. You're too"—he waved at her, grinning —"wholesome. And those freckles? They make me want to buy lemonade from your stand, or help you build a treehouse."

"Hey—" Her protest died when Dozer's face closed up. That was an expression he reserved for the presence of Miss Henatis, or, if she was unavailable, the devil incarnate.

In this case, there was not one demon, but three. "Hi, Wheezer. I know you're busy being mediocre, but do you think you could find the time to get Miss Henatis for me? Those drooling fossils won't move from the tables, and we want to sit there." Jessica jerked her chin at Danny and Miss Willie, who were absorbed in their books and magazines, quietly chatting. Britney and Ashley were in the unusual position of actually looking toward Livvy, although, true to form, their gaze went over her head, as if the simple act of recognizing her was beneath them.

"Well, if it isn't Malice in Wonderland." Dozer stood, radiating something more than simple anger. When Jessica stepped back, he smiled with a dark glee that made Livvy snicker. *Score one for the good guys.* "I'll go take care of it for you. I need you to take this folder to the boss. It's *critical.*" He put an empty manila envelope in her hands and stood, smoothing his pants as if going to do battle in a courtroom. "Follow me, witches, and I'll see to it that you're given every consideration toward getting the space you deserve."

Before the girls could muster a protest, Dozer strode briskly away, forcing them to follow him like obedient children. It was a lovely bit of theater on his part, with the added benefit that Lizzy could pretend to go on an errand and avoid any prolonged contact with them. She wasn't certain, but their attitudes were so vile she wondered if it was infectious. Livvy eased to her feet and began the slow walk with what she regarded as a stunt folder in one hand, the other trailing along a wall as a substitute for Dozer's hand.

Or Keiron's. His would be better. That brought a smile to her face, but it faded as she stopped before the ominously bland door of Miss Henatis' office. She raised her hand and knocked twice.

The door swung open silently.

Livvy spent her life obeying. It was what she'd done, mostly because she was, at heart, a good person who had like-minded people around her. Part of her willingness to follow orders was born of simple need. Often, she *had* to listen to her parents, or her doctors, or teachers. To do otherwise meant exposing herself to danger, since something as simple as a fright or the common cold could kill her. Her life had been lived on a precipice between safety and the unspoken prayer that somehow, Livvy would survive long enough to find a suitable heart. In the mean-time, she was a girl who tended to listen, and think, and obey.

This was not one of those times.

She flapped the empty folder against one hand, listening to the paper warble as the dark office spread before her. Inside, a near perfect blackness was broken only by the gleam of hallway light on glass, perhaps the cabinets filled with books and treasures untold. It gave her a thrill to think of that many unseen mysteries a mere light switch away. Without a thought, she reached around the corner and felt for the telltale plastic of a switch.

She found it. With a casual flick, she lifted the lever and sent the room into a blaze of harsh light from the sterile fluorescent panels above. They flickered lazily then stabilized with a series of random pops, as if waking from a long nap. A light smell of disinfectant curled through the air, and it was cold. Unusually cold, even for the library. Livvy shuddered at the temperature before taking a long look around the orderly space. Directly across from her gaze squatted an enormous desk that was more statement than furnishing. Its purpose was clear; when approaching, the vast sweep of polished wood was intended to leave no doubt as to the rank and station of the person sitting behind it. Livvy sneered at something as shallow as intimidation through a wide, plain desk, but then she knew little of Miss Henatis, other than a feeling of general unease. Other than a pen holder made from something like cardboard, the desk was clear.

The rumors were true. Museum quality books and oddities surrounded her in tortured rows of such order that there was a pervasive feeling of disuse and melancholy hanging around every dusty volume. Out on the library floor, there were books that seemed casually forgotten, but in here books of rare beauty were being squandered in a kind of literary purgatory. She saw epics, and poems, and illustrated books in languages that were completely unreadable, but amazing to behold nonetheless. If anything, their mystery only added to the appeal of each gilded spine behind glass that was so thick and old it was warped like slowly melting ice.

She recognized a series of medical texts in Latin, the spidery scrollwork on them vibrant in painted gold. As she got closer to the cabinets, Livvy was certain she could smell paper, and dust, and maybe even a hint of the years that had passed since someone took the time to capture thoughts of things both wondrous and factual. She was tempted to try one of the cabinet doors, but thought that discretion was the better part of valor in a space like Miss Henatis'.

A frisson of fear coursed through her at the thought of being caught, and with that she knew it was time to go. The treasures around her required a day, perhaps even a month in which to drink in their details, and that was time that she simply did not have. It was a mournful thing to turn away from the bookish delights, but she did it — and then bumped into a low table that she'd somehow missed. Livvy was transfixed. The table was rectangular, dull wood with a glass surface, like a lightbox.

And it was filled with smoke.

The vapors curled about in serpentine pleasures, whirling and eddying even as she watched. A gleam of opalescent light peeped from within the glass table, shifting and changing shapes like a blackbird's wing in the sun of a late spring day. It was magic. It was alive, of that she was certain. She reached to place a fingertip on the glass, but pulled it away with a hiss — at first.

It was colder than the silent depths of the ocean, and where her finger made contact, the smoke rushed to greet her in a hungry wave. Livvy knew fear then, in a way that was beyond any of the long nights in hospital where the only question on her mind was whether she would live or die. This — vapor, or whatever it was, did not want her life. It called to her soul, and she could hear it whisper through the glass with a sinister urging.

"What are you doing in here? Was I unclear? Is language a weak point for you?" The questions hit Livvy like a barrage of ice. Her heart jumped, she whirled, and for a dizzying moment, spots floated in front of her eyes as she put a questing hand out to stabilize herself lest she fall into the unknown mystery of that box filled with the hungriest thing she'd ever known.

Miss Henatis waited for her vision to clear before resuming her verbal assault. Her brows were knitted together and spots of color danced across her pale cheeks in a display of such unfiltered rage that Livvy wondered if she was, for the first time in her life, about to be hit by another human being. It was a wholly natural reaction, and she had to stifle a gasp of relief. An angry librarian was nothing compared to the wispy, unseen depths of something she knew to be evil.

"I'm so—so sorry, Miss Henatis. Dozer sent me to deliver—"

"Have I indicated that I care about what Dozer says? Or thinks? Perhaps he can offer me advice on delicate surgery or the position of the stars, wouldn't that be lovely, mmm?"

After an appropriate moment of penance, Livvy looked up, fighting hard not to cry. She wasn't scared. She was angry at letting herself be shooed away from three vapid girls who couldn't form an insult between them. Her moment of weakness before Dozer's good deed led her here, to being rounded on by a woman who had all of the personality of a dragon wearing cream-colored panty hose.

Fury bubbled up inside Livvy, replacing the cold dagger of fear that was splitting her chest only seconds earlier. *I am no child to be spoken to this way. Damn you, Dozer, I can fight for myself.*

"Did you just say something?" Miss Henatis' voice oozed derision before she laughed, a short, jagged sound like breaking glass. "I find it hard to believe that you've violated something as critical as the protection of my office, and now you have the audacity to be combative?" Her narrow head shook like a fox happening upon a lame rabbit, but then a calm fell over the woman, leaving her features placid once more. The transition took less than ten seconds, leaving the air between them flat with dismissal. It was robotic, and cold, and in the aftermath, Miss Henatis seemed to transition from human into something more like a facsimile of one.

For the second time in that office, Livvy shuddered, but her anger returned to warm her and she said, simply, "No, ma'am. I can assure you, I won't set foot in this room again."

As Livvy wove around a chair to the door, the librarian laughed, and this time there was nothing human about the sound at all. "I wouldn't be so certain of that."

The mist curled under the glass, making a noise like distant whispers in a rain-drenched forest. Miss Henatis smiled wetly as Livvy closed the door with a pointed click.

They sat knee to knee with a kind of familiarity that was gentle and warm. "So they call you Wheezer because . . . ?" Keiron asked, his face a mix of anger at the girls and pleasure at being so close to her. They were tucked in their alcove again, the thick book of ancient history on the floor next to them. Livvy held his hands, moving them back and forth, with a half-smile turning her lips into a bow. He had good hands, long and strong. They were male hands, so different from hers, without a hint of freckling or delicacy. Each finger was exotic to her senses, but also familiar, as if they were designed to twine together. There were pads of muscle underneath parts of each knuckle, and she took a small delight in running her own thumbs over the bulbs, tickling him lightly.

"I've had good years, and bad ones, too. We've gone to school together since we were kids. They weren't always like this. Just sort of happened over the years, until one day I walked into class and they decided, together, that I was the enemy. Something to be kicked around, I guess, and a lot of times I didn't feel well enough to fight back. I wasn't happy to be their punching bag, but some days it was hard enough just catching my breath." She looked away, sifting a bitter memory. "I think it was in eighth grade that Britney called me Wheezer. It stuck, but it was a lot better than the previous ones she'd gifted me. There was Spot, and Freckles, and Star Map." She shrugged. Livvy had been in an out of surgery so many times she'd lost count. A nickname was like getting a shot to her; it was a momentary jab, and then it was over.

"And yet you excel at school, don't you?" He was looking at her with his head tilted slightly. Behind him through the window, clouds swirled. It was going to snow again, and the clouds were gravid with mild threat.

She gave a grudging nod. "I have a lot of help."

"Oh?"

"Mom and dad are both — well, they're really smart, and they just sort of lead by example. Dad's always muttering into some sort of science book, and mom's just got this natural gift for languages. Between them, there wasn't really anything I couldn't ask about, and they were always there for me." She turned to him, her voice firming to reveal a side of her that was less a girl, and more the woman underneath. "I never felt like they were coddling me because of my health. They really were good people who happened to love me more than anything. I guess it might have been the whole only child thing, but still." Livvy smiled, and the angles faded with her ardent insistence.

He could see the effects of her upbringing in the way she spoke to him. To Dozer. Even her oddly gentle regard for the collection of misfits she called her regulars.

"What about you? Are you a scientist in the making? What about school?"

"I guess you would say I'm home schooled, but it's — well, we're rather intense in my family, and there were plenty of kids to compete against, but I'm the youngest. That's a whole different experience, since my parents were intensely concerned with our education. There was this kind of purpose to everything that we did as a family, but not in an unkind manner." His tone was accepting, even respectful.

Livvy understood. Her parents treated her in much the same way, offering to guide her without the use of threat or denial. It was more of a gentle insistence that she be given the things she needed to succeed, like a tide that was always lifting her and never leaving her behind.

"I get it. I mean, mom and dad are incredibly smart, but they relate to everyone. They see life through a lens of moments." She smiled at the memory of her father saying those exact words on more than one occasion.

"How so?" He was playing with her hands now.

A delicate flush rose in her chest at his attentions. Her answer was a kiss. It was swift, but soft, and her eyes glittered with unkempt laughter that curled her lips upward. There was joy in the kiss. "Like that. I wanted it, and it happened, and now we can think about it, but one thing we won't ever do is regret not having it as a memory. Because of this" — she looked down at her scar, its raised ridge an indictment of her flaw — "I don't believe in wasting time or letting things pass me by. I'm forced to plan, but that doesn't mean I'm not hungry for life and everything that comes with it." It was as close to a motto as she'd ever had, and it served her well. Livvy's mind was a bright and curious thing, even if her heart was weak. She learned to adjust her wishes on the fly, and to never miss out on the things she could do, when they were possible. With that thought, she leaned forward to kiss him again, but he met her in the middle.

This time they lingered, and she noticed a low-grade heat building in her face. Their lips fit together at a delicate tilt, parting only when she felt her chest rise slightly with the need to breathe. When she did, her senses filled with the closeness of him, and for a moment she forgot that they were in a library. Where she worked. With a boss who had a table that looked like a portal to hell. She kept that to herself, for some reason. Maybe it was just too weird to be shared, and so much of Livvy's life had been on the far side of normal. This time with Keiron was real, and she wouldn't risk it with something that seemed like it was from a waking dream.

"What day did you study kissing?" he teased, taking her hands again.

"I learned about it the same way I do all sports. In a book." Her grin was between coy and challenging, like her kisses. "By the way, when did you fall?" She felt bold in between his kisses. The way he looked at her made it real, even when her lips tingled with the touch of stars. Whatever was happening, it was more than her imagination could create. His hand touched her face, then ran down the curve of her neck to rest for a fluttering moment where her pulse beat, frantic with undiscovered things. "You know, for me?"

Keiron's laugh rang in the alcove as they became even more detached from whatever was going on around them. "I didn't fall. I was pushed." At her confusion, he tilted his head to look at her through his eyelashes. "The first time. This time? I fell. And what a landing." They learned something over the next few minutes. Even in a library, time stands still when your senses are filled with someone who treats you like spun gold, and in that moment, Livvy shone. After they slumped together, lips still tingling with memory, he sobered, looking around. "What about your boss? That — the mean one? Will she find you here?"

"You mean will she find *us* here? Maybe. Not sure I care." Just saying the words felt good, despite a responsible twinge. "I guess I should head back to the desk before Dozer sends out a search party." She looked around, frowning. "I feel like this is a little sanctuary. I don't really want to leave."

"I know." He did. There was a warmth to the air, brought on by their confessions, and stories, and kisses. It built a charge around them like a shell, and to leave it meant admitting that there was something out there other than the two of them. "Can I wait here, maybe?"

She pulled at her lip, nodding. "I don't see why not. I get another break, and then I'm done for the day."

He stood, pulling her to her feet. There was reluctance in his motion, but then she smiled and he was left with nothing to do but kiss her again. "I'll wait."

She made it five steps before her first look back. He was waiting. She smiled, despite the clouds and snow spreading before her through the windows. They could make their own sunshine.

CHAPTER SIXTEEN:

Grievance

He sergeant of guards was a rarity in Sliver; he wore no sleeves with his otherwise full combat armor, and every inch of his body was covered in rippling muscle. In a society that prized grace, he was a brutish figure with shaggy dark hair, a face like a thundercloud, and hands permanently crooked in the manner of the professional swordsman. When he stomped to the front of the stands, the silence that fell was immediate and tinged with fear.

"You will remain quiet while I speak, or I will personally remove you from this place." His growl invited no discussion or reaction, and with a final sweeping glare, he turned to the Factors who sat high above in their chairs, waiting for him to begin the proceedings. Angels were enthralled with ritual. This desire for rules allowed their society to flourish, if in a somewhat fearful manner, but it removed a great deal of the uncertainty that had ripped the world before theirs into a mass of squabbling races and nations. Now, there was only Sliver, and in the middle of that, The Grievance. It was here that the Factors could wield their enormous power, dividing, shaming, and stealing, all in the name of extending their rule for just one more day.

"Council, I give you your just due. The Grievance is yours." The sergeant, whose name was Horun, stepped back and rotated crisply, letting his gaze slide across Saiinov before beginning to settle into a pose where he could watch both council and crowd at once.

Saiinov inclined his head, one professional to another, but Horun ignored him, choosing to rake the assembled angels with a look that verged on active disgust. The guard was imperious and filled with a violence that simmered at the surface of his every gesture, but Saiinov paid him no need, knowing that truly dangerous beings didn't need to preen. Vasa stood slightly behind, arm linked with Habira in a unified front. They wore similar expressions of calm, though hints of excitement flared in Habira's youthful face. Only a stone or a corpse could ignore the energy that permeated The Grievance, as the air was charged with an atmosphere of expectation and indecision. Half the crowd wanted House Windhook to be punished in a spectacular manner, but the other half understood what was actually unfolding before them. It was the most direct assault on council authority that anyone in The Grievance could remember, and House Windhook had the added interest of being the aggressor. They not only thought they could win, but they were planning on doing so in the widest, most open forum possible. It was a small wonder that there were no seats to be found among the rustling wings of angels who knew that something critical was about to happen.

After a practiced delay in which the Factors let the

conversation burn out to a hum, Nera rapped her knuckles on the tall, sweeping table. "As you may have guessed, the contests will follow an established pattern that has been used since our wholly legitimate rule began nearly a thousand years ago."

This declaration was greeted with discreet coughs and murmurs at the rather generous terminology, since the Crescent Council had been called everything under the moon except *legitimate*. With a quelling look, the compact, aging Nera stood, letting her sleeves fall past her hands in a silken flutter. "Sword. Then spell. Then sword. Naturally, I will only be too happy to begin the proceedings. Horun, bring the insolent pup to the circle and see that she awaits my arrival." With that, Nera began the long, curved walk down from the dais where she ruled, as Horun pointed to the center of the wide, smooth floor with an aggressive jab of his finger.

His gesture was just short of a threat, leaving Habira no doubt as to the climate she would be fighting in. "You will have no Wingrider for this contest, as it is one of the two preliminaries. At the discretion of the council, only your father will be allowed to have his flank guarded during the resolution of your imaginary charges." His lip curled in a sneer that was so practiced, Habira laughed at him as she walked past to the slightly depressed ring that indicated the outer edge of the combat area. Countless feet had worn a groove where fighters had won or lost over the centuries, their crimes and complaints all but lost to the ravages of time.

A sense of purpose and history began to infuse Habira, who was naturally prone to emotional reactions. With a glance to her mother and father, she unsheathed her sword, a beautifully simple weapon with a plain hilt of wrapped hide and an edge that could make clouds weep. It was longer than her arm, of middle weight, and adorned only with her initials; a gift of her parents when it became apparent that fighting would be as natural to her as flying.

Nera took her time, confident and well-schooled in the importance of theatrics. She was of average height, but solidly built and graced with the carriage of an aging athlete. Her severe hair was pulled back into a dark knot that matched her boots and bracers in a color so forgettable it was neither brown nor black. She disrobed to reveal light armor in graduated tones of brown; the Windbeast hide had been sewn from strips that conformed to her aging body, yet still managed to convey a sense of competence and danger. When she smiled at Habira, her teeth were square and rimed with the residue of wind herbs, but her face was unlined and there was no doubt that she wore the experience of a warrior with ease. Nera's eyes were too dark to be called green, verging into a shifting hazel that seemed to make her even more menacing, if it were possible. It was Nera's bland nature that set Habira's alarms ringing, for Saiinov had explained over the years that the best fighters are rarely the most intimidating.

"You will assume a ready stance in the appropriate locations." Horun stood, feet apart in an aggressive posture. There was an air of anticipation about him, although it was not due to the oncoming combat. Rather, he wanted nothing more than an excuse to attack or disqualify Habira for ignoring one of the arcane rules that governed the fighting grounds of The Grievance. When she smiled pleasantly and took her place without comment, he nearly growled with disappointment.

Habira placed her boots in divots worn from countless other combatants who had driven forward from the same spot, launching themselves into the fight with abandon. As a child of House Windhook, there would be no headlong rush or wild swinging of her weapon. She felt a chill of concentration slide down her spine, masking the natural nervousness that rippled across her awareness. The next moments would go far in determining the fate of the skies, but more importantly, her own life. She had no doubt that Nera would go for the kill; there would be no investigation into an accidental death, and none would have proceeded, anyway. The council would snuff out House Windhook, and then their memory.

If they could.

"Address the council." Horun's command was cold and directed fully at Habira.

As one, she and Nera raised their arms in salute, while dipping on one knee in a fluid, practiced motion that imparted respect and readiness. The stands began to rustle again as excitement spilled over, heedless of any possible retribution on the part of Horun or the other guards who even now shot fearsome glances at random angels who dared to comment on the proceedings.

"Child of mine, you shall win." Saiinov's words were low and heard only by Habira, who drank them in with a single, terse nod of appreciation.

Nera looked at her with careful disinterest, revealing nothing other than a general air of intolerance at the presence of the younger, vibrant woman before her.

There was no warning given. Horun waved a hand between them and stepped back, the hint of a smile curving his lips as his hands settled on the pair of swords he wore, declaring his authority over the area.

Nera moved first, slipping to the left and bringing her sword before her in a midlevel position. The blade was thin, long, and curved slightly, sacrificing two edges for the added reach and narrow tip, which could be used for stabbing at a distance. The handle was squat and hewn from the bone of a creature that had been powerfully built; Nera's hand closed around the grip with the familiarity of a lover. These were details that anyone would have seen, but Habira was not waiting to receive the attack without gathering her own impressions as well.

She noticed that Nera chose the longer weapon due to her short arms and a possible old injury that limited her range of motion in the neck. Immediately, Habira skittered hard to the side, forcing Nera to turn and follow. It was as the young warrior expected; Nera would have to anticipate such moves and begin her turn prior to any actual movement from her opponent. They circled once before reversing their direction in a smooth union that was not unlike a partnered dance; both of them stood light on their feet with an economy of motion. There was no waving of swords or twitching about like nervous children in a school time brawl; if anything, both women seemed on the verge of losing interest in the fight, so complete was their masking of any tactical decisions.

Then Nera struck. She moved like a predatory beast, bringing her blade straight forward in a motion so fast that the blade seemed to lengthen in her hands. At full extension, she remained perfectly balanced, only falling back when the blow was turned by Habira with a desperate twist of her midsection. The ringing report ended in a metallic thunk as Nera's blade ended its arc at the handguard of Habira's sword. They broke apart to resume their carefully measured stalking, but this time both women regarded each other differently. The fight was real, the atmosphere charged by the gasps of the angels in the stands. Only Saiinov remained completely silent — along with the combatants. Everywhere else, conversations erupted like small fires, skipping from spot to spot as the attendees felt the need to add their own fuel to the event that everyone had seen only seconds earlier. The sun continued to stream down in a cloudless sky, piercing through the arcing spires of The Grievance. There were few shadows and little wind as they were protected from the elements, despite being in the vast open air of Sliver's innermost environs.

Habira was brimming with youth and in excellent condition. Her hours of endless sparring with Saiinov would pay off, but only if she could extend the contest into one of attrition through exhaustion. Nera was no fool. She would press the issue, hoping to cause a mistake, or perhaps using her greater experience to force Habira into a decision that she would instantly regret. They began their slow circle, but it quickly ended when Habira took matters into her own hands. She turned hard against the direction of their motion, forcing Nera to twist her body in a single, rigid column. With a hiss, Habira's sword struck out to slash cruelly down the length of Nera's exposed midsection. It was a long, shallow cut, parting armor and skin but doing little real damage.

The wound did change Nera's mind about her opponent. Bleeding freely, the Factor who had won dozens of battles now looked at the upstart woman through narrowed eyes. She hadn't seen the strike coming, and even if she had, she would not have been capable of parrying the attack directed specifically at her weak side. It was a kind of fighting known to some Easterners, but not widely practiced. That meant Nera was essentially unguarded, and would be forced to present a single side and fight in a fencer's posture, thus limiting her ability to do real damage unless she could wound Habira with a stabbing motion.

Nera was far from knowing just a single trick; she had not advanced to her position of power without being a viable threat with both her mind and blade in endless variations. If she had to fence, then so be it. She leaned her body slightly back as they began to address each other, the tedious circling no longer possible since Nera followed Habira motion for motion. The two women began to let their wings rustle slightly as nerves and combat took a toll on their outward calm, but it was minimal noise and distraction. They were both too good, despite their age difference. Saiinov and Vasa's work was on display with every liquid move that Habira made to counter any attempt at pinning her to a frontal attack.

Nera lunged but did not strike. Rather, she held her blade back for the inevitable counter-stroke, deftly turning Habira's blade out and down with minimal effort. It was a mistake, though, because Habira never intended to cut her opponent; not in the midst of such an obvious trap. With a blur, Habira's left foot shot forward to kick Nera directly over the cut from their first engagement, eliciting a hiss of pain as the Factor was forced to tuck and roll, lest she lose her head to Habira's seamless follow up with her sword. In a controlled rush, Habira leapt ahead, slashing once at Nera's back. Feathers parted without resistance as the left wing was reduced to a stump of quills, waving feebly from the shock of the cut.

A roar burst from the crowd at such evil. Among the angels, their wings were sacred. Was it not the gift of flight that set them apart from the people who had crawled, mired to the planet, only to be wiped away in a series of disasters so gruesome that there was little to be found of their presence? Had angels not evolved to fill the need for justice and reason, and if that were true, then what was an angel without wings? Shrieks of protest rolled over Habira as she followed up her first stroke with a second, this one slicing deep into the upraised, defensive palm of the Factor, whose expression quickly became both mortal and scared.

Nera bucked upward, using her compact legs as a jackhammer to lift Habira up and away in a flailing tangle, too low to open her wings and gasping for air from the force of the blow. She landed with the barest hint of control, rolling across one shoulder to a sitting position. Her right leg was bent at an angle that could only mean one thing: she'd broken it in the violent fall and would have to meet Nera on one foot.

Or, she could yield.

A slick of sweat burst onto Habira's skin, causing her father to momentarily look away at the sight of his child in such pain. He was a warrior, as was she, but in his mind she was still the precocious child who he'd taught to fly less than four decades earlier. Like a beast shaking off the arrow of a Skywatcher, Habira stood, rolling her head from side to side with a delicacy that meant she was close to losing consciousness.

Nera attacked. In one step, she closed the gap and led with the tip of her blade, hoping to pierce the grimacing Habira before she could regain her faculties and assume any kind of defensive posture. Their bodies crashed together with a muffled thud, sending Habira into a dangerous lean as she reached back with her left arm hoping to brace herself for the inevitable impact. Nera didn't relent, opting instead to continue forward and use the weight of her body as a weapon, swinging her sword arm wide to bring the blade inward toward Habira's ribcage for a killing blow. Any pretense of surrender or battle decorum was gone; the crowd seemed to sense this and began urging Nera to finish the fight. Their cries rose in a crescendo of violence, charging the air further with a bloodlust that was primal and thick.

Habira drew her knees up in a motion she'd been taught as a child; it created a gap between their bodies that was wide enough for Nera to suffer an elbow to the side of her jaw. The crack of teeth was audible to the highest stands, sending a new ripple of shouts across The Grievance as the need for blood ratcheted ever higher. Habira rolled, screamed in pain at the motion of her leg, and lashed out with the handle of her sword to add another punishing blow to Nera's face, this time on the unprotected right side. Pain exploded in Nera's skull, leaving her stunned and gasping as Habira took three halting steps away, turned, and brandished her weapon in a reasonable posture. She swayed but seemed alert.

The same could not be said for Nera, who fought valiantly to shake the cobwebs from her mind. The two blows left her dizzy and weak, her sword arm slumping dangerously toward the ground. She was open to attack, and she knew it. With a grunt of effort, she lifted her blade higher as the intelligent gaze returned to her face. They weren't done. Not yet.

Neither woman uttered a word, nor did they plan on it. Theirs was a combat designed with two vastly different goals in mind. Nera wanted to embarrass the younger fighter, and by extension, her house. Habira wanted to defrock the Factor who she saw as a priestess of an evil religion; one that robbed people of freedom and sought only to further its own existence.

Carefully, Habira put her foot down, testing its reliability on the bone-slick fighting circle. Her body language said it was good enough, but she remained in place, opting to force Nera to her, preferably in a frontal attack, although a quiver of pain rippled upward to shake her wings in a sign that her reserves were failing fast.

Nera took what was given, moving to the right and inviting Habira to open her sword arm out, leaving the midsection of her body exposed to the more seasoned fighter's inevitable attack. Habira rotated, hissing in pain, then began to tumble slowly inward, her leg collapsing to the side as the battered knee began to fail. She flapped her wings in frustration, but they were too slow to open. There would be no saving hover, no miraculous leap upward to launch her into a victorious dive that overwhelmed the grounded Nera, whose own wings moved reflexively as she thought of the same attack. In a clatter of blades, they met, with Habira slumping to one side under the onslaught of a superior strength and inertia. She began the inevitable fall, trying to twist herself in yet another saving move that would stop her from slamming into the circle with the last act of her life. If she hit the floor, there would be no rising, as Nera was too close and too skilled to miss another opportunity.

Habira threw her sword away then grabbed Nera

with both hands and flipped her deftly around so that the Factor became a cushion for her well-placed fall. The sword that had been bearing down on her chest was now wildly out of position, and once again Habira used her knees to drastic effect as they slammed into Nera's stomach, causing the older, smaller woman's arms to draw protectively inward. Habira wrenched the sword from Nera's hand, completed the roll across her body, and found herself squatting directly behind the dazed and bleeding angel who had only seconds earlier been plotting a death blow. With a dismissive flick of her wrist, Habira removed both of Nera's wings in their entirety then ran the sword through her shoulder and pushed it forward until the Factor was pinned, like an insect, to the ground.

In the chaos that erupted, Habira turned to Saiinov and smiled. "How was that, Father?"

His answering grin was malicious. "Better than we practiced, dear. They never saw it coming." With meaning, he looked at Horun, and then the council members in turn before helping his daughter to her feet. The limp, while present, was minimal, sending waves of rage through the council at their use of deception. Utipa tried to hide a smile of admiration, but failed, drawing a murderous glare from Ophaniel, who considered such tactics to be nothing short of criminal. With her own wintry look, Utipa turned from her wizened counterpart to stare at Saiinov. Anyone watching could see the calculations behind her deliberately bland gaze as she alone began to put the elements of the story before her into some kind of order. Whether or not she understood the grander scheme of House Windhook was irrelevant, as she was neither fighting nor willing to share her wisdom on the matter.

Utipa was not alone in her curiosity at the swift and brutal nature with which Nera had been beaten. True, she'd wounded Habira with relative ease, but it seemed almost planned, as if the young Skywatcher had a pre-set level of damage she was willing to incur in order to render Nera overconfident and vulnerable. Another deeply troubling fact hidden in the post-fight chaos was the lack of secrecy on Saiinov's part. He'd done nothing to hide their planned misdirection, meaning that he had no concern for any repercussions. Saiinov — and by extension, House Windhook — was planning on victory, and their actions proved a confidence that should have frightened the council.

Whatever the plan, it had been simple, elegant, and effective. Nera would be years in recovery, with her reputation left in even greater tatters than the fibrous remains of her wings. It would be difficult, if not impossible, for her to rule again, and a seat on the council was hardly an appointment for life. Allowing her to maintain her position would show weakness on the part of the remaining Factors, who, with the exception of the arrogant Castiel, were all privately wondering exactly how many more of them would fall before the day was over.

"The second issue will be concluded in" — Horun squinted up into the sun, calculating — "ten minutes. If there is any deviation form established decorum, the penalty will be instantaneous. There will be no second warning."

"We wouldn't dream of sullying the pristine reputation of this fine place, Horun." Saiinov's teeth were exposed, but there was no mirth in his expression. He stared hard at the bulky sergeant until their gaze was interrupted by movement on the dais. Ophaniel was in motion, an air of disgust about him that could be felt even at a distance as his astronomer's robe moved about him like a lazy black curtain. The stars and symbols covering the garment moved around, some flaring into a glow, and others vanishing into the folds of fabric like shy children. His long pink hands moved with anticipation of his task as he brought his sparse, ancient frame to the circle without ever taking his eyes from Saiinov.

"I cannot thank you enough for this, Windhook." Ophaniel seemed genuinely pleased, his long teeth bared in a smile that transformed his face into a mask of vengeful lust. What hair he had left was snow white and waving about his dark, battered skin, giving him an appearance that looked on the verge of madness. His robe was open at the throat, revealing a sparse patch of grizzled hair, which he scratched at absently before clearing his lungs and spitting outside the circle in a complete breach of decorum. Horun said nothing, leaving the disgusting old Factor to his crude preparations.

"I see your manners are sparkling as ever, Ophaniel." Vasa appeared at Saiinov's side, having stepped forward from the shadows next to the nearest section of seats. She was clothed simply in a robe of Windhook colors, blue and silver. A thin, woven belt of white fabric was knotted at her waist, giving the elegant woman an appeal that made Ophaniel seem nothing short of monstrous by comparison. "Your blow was well struck, daughter. And now, let us bring this second issue to a close, shall we?" Vasa's face transformed from a beautiful matriarch into that of a stalking predator as she stepped, unbidden, to the edge of the circle. With a hand, she silenced Horun before he could speak. "You'll not bully me, regardless of your position. If you interfere in this proceeding in any manner, I'll have your tongue, for a start. You won't like the rest of the story, sergeant."

Horun's fists curled, but Ophaniel laughed. He saw her insults as an added spice to what he was going to do to Vasa, and by extension, her house. But mostly to Vasa, for her beauty and confidence were traits that wriggled under his skin like an army of worms, and he could not wait to lay her low.

Vasa kissed Saiinov as the crowd's need to speak overcame their fears of reprisal. "If I fall, you know what to do."

His answering nod was short, but decisive.

"This will be the second issue, and it will be decided now. You may step forward to receive my punishment," Ophaniel called out in a surprisingly strong, if high, voice. His announcement was a tonic to the crowd, who began to fall silent as Vasa walked around the circle, away from Ophaniel, and took her place where Nera stood only moments earlier.

Horun resumed his previous position as well, looking slightly less arrogant than he had at the beginning of Vasa's contest. These opponents were not behaving at all like they should, in his experience. There was no hesitancy, or negotiation, or even grim acceptance of their spectacular destruction before the council, and the first fingers of unease began to curl around his spine like the touch of a lonely spirit. With a visual shake, he cleared his blocky, martial head and lifted one hand, positioned with the menace of a falling blade.

The sun went behind a cloud, casting the first of many

shadows, and Horun said simply, "Begin."

A bolt of sizzling red light flew toward Vasa, taking the entire crowd by surprise as no one had even seen Ophaniel move. As a master Scholar, he'd readied a punishing glyph prior to even approaching the circle, and he released it the instant he could do so without fear of looking like a scheming bully, which he was.

It missed. Vasa was there, and then she was gone, fading into a wisp of stars that regrouped several feet away, well safe from the hideously powerful spell that would have rendered her into ashes. The gasp from angels low and high in the stands overwhelmed the curses spat by Ophaniel, who lost the advantage, surprise, and a considerable amount of energy with his initial attack.

Vasa emerged from the nether with a look of grim satisfaction; where her daughter had been smug, she was focused, and leaving no doubt that her efforts against the older, more experienced Factor would be free of playful discourse. To Vasa, the fight was nothing more than business, but with stakes that were incredibly high. Scholars understood that offense and defense did not mesh well; so it was no surprise when Vasa moved again, this time to the left, her hands rotating in a lazy arc around each other, fingers waving like tendrils of wind herbs in the open sky. In the space between, filaments of white light began to build, spinning into a loose blossom of crackling energy that faded in and out of the visible spectrum. She was a master among Scholars, but within that elite association she had no equal when it came to the use of Timeslip.

The widening globe of energy that Vasa created seemed to hesitate, then stabilized in the form of a whirling disc the size of a warrior's shield. It was thin and gauzy, and it let light through in a warped vision that twisted the space behind her into a folly of shadows and shapes. Sneering with delight, Ophaniel didn't know the exact glyph she was using, but he recognized defense when he saw it.

He struck again, this time with a cone of magnificent orange flamelets that spat wild showers of sparks as they hurled themselves toward Vasa like a mass of wasps. They dove and swooped and spun about in an oddly cheerful dance that would have been beautiful had it not been one of such dangerous intent. The entire cloud of fiery nodes crossed the space between them in less than the time that a person could blink twice. A storm of tiny flames slammed into Vasa's defensive shield in unending waves until the last stragglers were enveloped in the white light with small, audible *whuffs*.

The spell vanished, consumed by Vasa's shield without any lingering sign. The impact of such a transformation of energy left her swooning, but she righted herself and stomped one booted foot against the floor of the circle. From the point of impact, a line of disruption took shape through sound and shadow, forming and re-forming in an advancing braid of darkly twisting whispers that reached Ophaniel with a sound of satisfaction. He was hurled upward, robes fluttering in a blinking twirl as his symbols winked in and out of existence while they attempted to absorb the powerful assault on his body. Vasa's spell was not designed to kill, it was built to deconstruct, a form of magic so primal that there would be nothing left of Ophaniel, save the scraps of his arrogant robe.

The cagey Factor wove his own defense, causing the

fatal magic to curl around him in the wispy shapes of a distant fire. With a cackle of triumph, he landed, spry for his years, to stand glaring at Vasa as the remaining lights of magical discharge popped into nothingness around him.

"Clever, but futile." Ophaniel was not prone to boasting, but he could still admire a capable Scholar who dared to oppose him. At least such admiration was possible until the moment of their destruction, which would be soon if he had anything to say in the matter. He let his glyph speak next, raising both hands, fingers intertwined and rigidly outward like a cage. The air rippled between him and Vasa. His effort pulled on the fabric of air, an elemental magic of old words and power that only the vain or savvy dared to shape.

Vasa knelt, arms crossed in a classic defensive posture. She made her decision; if she could survive this ancient attack, then the fight would continue, but she would not squander any more energy through costly defensive spells. Her lips moved in a low chant as the warped atmosphere of Ophaniel's casting flowed over and around her, seeking an opening anywhere that it might pierce her natural resistance and scramble her innards like a dropped egg. As a Scholar, Vasa's decades of rigorous practice came into play, but she was still susceptible to the onslaught. A tendril of shimmering nothingness punctured her armor with a wet tear, lifting her from the ground like a toy as her arm went rigid with shock and pain. Vasa's scream of agony echoed across The Grievance in confirmation of the battle; what went on in the circle was nothing less than war, and the first victim had been claimed. Gasps of fear and horror were interrupted by bloodthirsty cheers from the stands as angels declared their allegiance with ringing shouts or covered mouths. She fell with a crash within the confines of the circle, her arm twisted outward across one wing. White feathers, now scorched and smoking, drifted down on her still form as Saiinov knelt outside the circle, straining at the damnable confines of their rules of engagement.

Ophaniel crooked his pink fingers in glee, a smile of unabashed menace spreading across his face. He didn't look at the fallen Vasa, but saved his wicked celebration for Saiinov, who paid no heed to the preening Factor and his laughing sergeant who stood a few feet away, savoring every flare of her pain.

Vasa groaned, rolling over as blood ran freely from her mouth in a crimson stream. With the effort of a wounded beast, she dragged herself to a crouch, one knee down and her hands spread before her on the circle to add stability. Even so, she swayed dangerously, her eyes a bleary mess of hurt and confusion.

"I am older than you, and so is my connection to all that a Scholar should know. You will die as you lived, a footnote of —"

A torrent of tiny flames burst from the ripping sky behind Ophaniel, driving straight ahead and setting him ablaze with the light of a dying sun. They pecked and nipped and seared at his wings, breaking through into the fabric of his astronomer's robe and then, in a wave of hideous crackling, opening the skin of his back to worry their way into his most secret places. His scream was a guttural rasp of pain and anger, as he writhed a half turn before the fire overtook him, sending him sprawling to the floor of the circle in a glittering mass of winking fires that flickered and died, just as he did.

Vasa stood, her every move one of dangerous imbalance, then walked forward to place one small foot on the blackened chest of the dead Factor. "You can master all things save one, filthy creature. You cannot master time." She smiled in a grimace of pain at Saiinov, who hovered at the circle's limit. "But I can." She made it four steps to the edge, and fell.

Saiinov caught her, cooing in her hair, his face contorted with fear for the woman who had found, crafted, and loosed a glyph of Timeslip to turn Ophaniel's own magic against him in the near future. "You are magnificent, my bride." Tears fell to her skin from his eyes, each one streaking the dusty cheeks of her pale skin. Together, they had earned those tracks of victory and pain, and Saiinov felt a dangerous anger take root in his core at what had been done to the woman who meant more to him than life itself. She was mother to his children, advisor to his dreams, and conscience to his martial side, often shaping his emotions to a higher and better plane than what he may have chosen. Together, they made the decision to crush a system that would use angels like disposable souls, and they knew it would have a high cost. First, they gave their son. Now, she gave her blood.

Saiinov handed his wife to Cressa, who looked utterly lost. "Hold her until help arrives. Do not let anyone touch her. If you do, I'll kill them. And then — you'll answer to me." There was no heat in his voice, only the cold, methodical declaration of a husband who was covered with his wife's blood. It was the tolling of a bell, like a distant warning, and Cressa accepted it in full, settling into a resting position so that she could tip a shell of cool water into Vasa's mouth. With small sips, the victorious Scholar and lady of House Windhook began to normalize her breathing, though her eyes were still hooded by occasional jolts of naked pain. After a moment in which Saiinov stalked to the circle, Vasa could sit. A moment after that, her eyes began to clear as she implored Cressa to move her safely back from the circle. Vasa wanted to be close, but not in the line of fire, as another blow to her battered frame might be fatal.

With a delicacy she hadn't shown before, Cressa lifted Vasa's unyielding frame, trying hard not to cause any more pain. She succeeded in moving her, but failed to do it without Vasa letting a small yip of hurt escape as she tucked her legs under into a sitting position. The noise had been . . . young, that was it, thought Cressa. It was the sound of a child, and just then she began to grasp how much damage Ophaniel had done to Vasa during their fight. She lay a protective hand lightly on Vasa's shoulder, feeling an upwelling of her own anger that this woman, who had been nothing but kind, was freely bleeding while her husband prepared to battle a swordsman of such repute that the outcome was a forgone conclusion.

Forgone for everyone except House Windhook's patriarch. He still looked angry, but there was a chill falling over him as he made his way silently to the circle. Horun had no chance to speak at all this time, as he was cut off with an imperious wave by Castiel, who looked nearly giddy at that the prospect of meeting and dispatching one of the council's greatest enemies. It was, in Cressa's young mind, a mistake. Castiel saw the blood and heard the noises of pain that seeped from Vasa, but he wasn't grasping the bigger picture.

Everything was riding on his performance.

Castiel was a gifted killer — crafty, strong, and

blessed with a natural guile that made him lethal to everyone he'd met in the circle, but never with such stakes. Looking at the immensely competent Saiinov, Cressa knew that an opponent of this caliber had never crossed blades with Castiel before, nor had the swaggering Factor been exposed to someone who drew from so many different fighting styles. Saiinov wasn't just a swordsman, he was a student — a scientist, a perfectionist of military sciences who believed that drawing from all useful sources would render a fighter that much more difficult to kill.

In his decades of rule as a Factor, Castiel had met and embarrassed his share of foes, although no one in the stands could actually recall the last time a challenger had actually put metal to the body of the elusive Factor and his whirling, slashing style of fighting. He was active, and athletic, and ruthless.

Horun's hand fell as a collective intake of breath marked the gravity of the final match. Saiinov and Castiel leapt forward in a dash of speed and power that left the crowd gasping. Kneeling next to her mother, Habira felt her heart catch at the display of sword craft that unfolded in that first blinding attack. She shook her head, humbled by an earlier thought that it would be she, and not her father, who would meet Castiel in the circle. The version of Saiinov fighting now was another animal entirely; his body moved like lightning in a blurring series of counters that Castiel had clearly intended to badly wound the challenger. There was no dancing or wasted movement; both Castiel and Saiinov saved energy as if their lives could be snuffed out with the slightest miscalculation.

Naturally, they were right.

Their longswords whispered through strokes of such

speed that Habira found it difficult to follow, even though her entire mind was focused on each movement. Cressa knelt, transfixed and silent. No one dared breathe unless it was absolutely necessary, save Vasa, who was using deep, calculated breathing to restore some degree of normalcy to her state of wellbeing. He darted a hand up to Cressa and pressed something into the surprised Flyer's hand.

"Lady?" She looked down at the small tile of bone, or shell—it could have been either. It was luminously thin and marked with a single, compact glyph in a language Cressa had never seen before.

Habira paid no heed to the exchange, watching the continuing fight unfold before them instead.

"When this is over, you must get to the southern aerie, one street over. You know the place? It's the widest, and least used landing space." Vasa spoke in a low, urgent tone, but her voice was reasonably strong. She would survive, it seemed. Fresh blood dripped from her nose and mouth after the declaration. She wiped at it impatiently, her dark eyes flickering with suppressed pain. Even with her grievous wounds, there was a regal nature that Cressa found compelling. She nodded, but her agreement was tenuous. Sensing this, Vasa elaborated, "Keiron is brave and clever, but he's no Scholar. I am the one who found the references to Timeslip and piercing the light of days. It was my spell that binds the ability to that tile in your hand. Look around you, Flyer. These guards will be overwhelmed when Saiinov wins."

At that, her husband began to make good on his word, scoring a hit on the leading arm of Castiel, who looked horrified at being wounded. The sensation of spilling his own blood was clearly new to the arrogant Factor, who launched a reprisal that Saiinov deftly turned with a clever downstroke that forced Castiel back in a stagger.

"It won't be long now. You'll arrive without your wings, and it's going to be — you're going to be confused. It's unlike anything you can imagine, Cressa. Do you understand? That tile will take you to within wingspans of my son, but you must be cautious. You have friends there, but even they cannot protect you from the vagaries of chance. There is danger. But you must listen to me now if you want to be redeemed." Vasa grabbed a fistful of gray feathers and pulled them savagely. "You can come back without these, but it takes an act of pure sacrifice. There, not here. Give them your heart, and you may return here." Tears spangled Vasa's eyes, her face stricken with turmoil. For the first time in her life, the Scholar had knowingly told a lie. "Go. Save him. Please. And we will save you." The world around them began to come apart at the seams.

A shout burst forth from the circle. Castiel suffered another wound, this time on his foot. Two of his toes remained where he'd been a moment earlier, and he was limping badly. Saiinov was breathing heavily, but looked fresh compared to the bedraggled, wounded Factor whose wings now dropped toward the ground. Saiinov's strategy seemed to be winning through subtracting Castiel's body parts. The crowd grew restless. They clearly hadn't considered the possibility that Saiinov — and House Windhook — might prevail. Neither had the dozens of guards, who began a not-so-discreet meander toward the street openings. Only Horun remained unmoved, for to falter would be nothing less than a death sentence, and the veteran guard knew it.

"Where am I going?" Cressa's plaintive question was

underscored by her youth, causing Habira to reach out and take her shoulder. Until that point, it hadn't seemed that she was paying any attention to the low tones between Vasa and the confused young Blightwing.

"You're going back. To get my brother, and if that doesn't work, to get her." Habira looked grim, as if neither choice was safe. Or possible.

"Who is *her*?" Now Cressa's confusion was total. She wanted redemption, but not if it meant death. She had no lust to end her life, no matter how noble the cause. Questions swirled. She *had* seen Vasa manipulate time. She knew it could be done.

The crowd saw the opening before Castiel knew he'd created it. Bleeding, gasping for air, and with flagging will, he repositioned his feet to a solid stance, knowing that anything less would result in being taken by Saiinov's boundless limits of speed and power. As he turned to place one boot behind the other, Saiinov came straight forward in a purely eastern move, his sword rotated in a tight half-circle to ring against the hilt of Castiel's battered sword. Bright scars on the hilt told a story of many strikes just like this one, but the savage punch that followed Saiinov's release of his sword took Castiel squarely in the nose, crunching flesh and bone alike in a devastating impact. Before the blade could fall, Saiinov kicked it back into his free hand and drove the sword into the meat of Castiel's thigh, making the Factor scream with agony that had been heard many times in the bloodied ground of the circle.

But not, the crowd thought as one, from the throat of a Factor. Their volcanic cheers began as Saiinov withdrew the blade, wiping it on Castiel's armor with a disdainful swipe.

"Habira," Vasa said, her tone dark. She took Cressa's hands in hers, looking the young Flyer in the eyes with a mix of apology and shame. "I'm sorry, Cressa. But it has to be this way."

Habira's sword cut the Flyer's wings off cleanly, leaving her nearly blind with pain and shock. She screamed, beginning to fall but propped up viciously by Habira, who shoved her toward the exits without mercy.

"Go! Leap! The Timeslip will unspool, all you must do is jump!" Habira was shouting as the stands began to empty. Panic broke free in a wild tangle of cries and running feet. There was no going back from the shattered edge of reason now that the scent of fear was in the air.

Sick with agony, Cressa staggered away into the growing streams of angels leaving The Grievance as quickly as they could. Some took wing, and others began to shove in a primal way, having lost their veneer of civilization at the first signs of trouble. Cressa vanished into the crowd, her future unknown. It was up to her now, and not even the power of House Windhook could help her decide what she would do. She would stay, and be crushed in the spiral of violence, or she would jump, and be asked to give her heart for a cause that was new and distant to her. The choices were clear. And not.

Saiinov began to leave the circle, but Horun leapt in front of him, spitting with rage. "You filth. You and your house end here, and it starts with this —" His sword rang on Saiinov's own, brought up in a flash of silver once it became apparent that the last remaining guard was going to avenge the council. As the remaining Factors began to run, all dignity lost, The Grievance started shaking with a seismic roar. There were too many feet, and too much panic.

The slender spires waved uncertainly above, throwing dangerous, moving shadows that only added to the scene of violent departure. When the top of one spire snapped off, if crashed down to crush a triad of angels who were poised to take flight, unleashing a new howl of fear that swept through the mob like cloudfire.

Habira pulled a coughing Vasa to her feet as Saiinov shouted above the destruction. "Leave us and you may live. That's the offer, and it won't be repeated." Saiinov held his sword at the ready, quietly hoping that Horun would choose valor over vengeance. He was wrong.

What Castiel used in the circle was elegance personified compared to the animal rush of Horun, who came forward without a hint of style or deceit. His massive arms brought the longsword he carried down in a blur —

— But Saiinov was gone, leaping up and over the towering angel to strike down at him with the end of his blade. It penetrated deep into the bulk of Horun's shoulder, cracking bone and prying apart sinews in a wicked cut that took the sergeant to his knees. As the guard fell, he lashed out with a massive fist, driving the blow into Saiinov's waiting ribs as he descended from his leap. Saiinov fell to the ground with a thud as the air left him like a ghost. An audible grating spoke of broken ribs, but he rolled, face white with pain, to bring his weapon up in a defensive posture.

Mortally wounded, Horun rose, lumbered forward, and swung wildly once again, but with far less power and accuracy. It was Habira who turned his blade, flicking it away with practiced ease. Her muscle memory disarmed Horun, but it was her mercy that cut him down with a single, hissing stroke to end his pain. She stood over the body, looking young and vulnerable despite the scene of apparent victory.

"Come, daughter. We need to get to the highest point now that the Factors have abandoned their posts." Saiinov held out a hand to his wife, who sagged into him with relief. As a triad, they began to push and shove through the maelstrom of fevered angels who knew that The Grievance was in the midst of a complete breakdown in order. Punches and kicks flew as angels leapt into motion, wings beating in frantic tempos to lift them up and away, or be pulled down into brawls that surged across the open spaces like schools of enraged Windbeasts. Everywhere, there was fighting, screams, and debris as Habira and Saiinov began to lay about with the flat of their swords, clearing a path as best they could.

After agonizing minutes of uncertainty and disarray, they clambered to the abandoned post of the Factors. The tall chairs, once seats of nobility, were now empty testaments to the weakness and cowardice of the Crescent Council.

All save one.

"You were always too clever by half, Windhook." Factor Utipa was smiling as yet another spire came crashing to the floor nearby, sending shards of bone and stone streaking outward in a lethal spray of shrapnel. She never moved, even as a wicked spear of glimmering debris split the air mere inches above her head. "You must have planned this for decades. I should have seen it coming when you challenged us so directly by convincing your son to travel back to—well, you know where he went. And you know that he can't be allowed to come back here despite your willingness to end life as we know it." Her black eyes shone with respect. And anger. Her hair whipped about in the unsteady winds that were building within The Grievance. The storm that had been brewing for so long had arrived, and no one standing there on the dais seemed surprised.

"He is coming back, and this place will welcome him." Saiinov's words were like iron, his gray eyes lit from within with the same certainty that the Factors possessed when they were sneering at his family from their lofty perches only moments earlier. In an instant, their fortunes were turned. Now, Utipa stood before them, her intentions uncertain, just like her future.

Utipa looked around calmly, even as a pair of angels streaked past to smash headlong into a slumping section of wall. The Grievance was emptying, but not without cost. Still forms lay sporadically on the wide expanse around them, the wings broken and bloodied. Not everyone was getting out. "Sliver won't fall, despite your efforts. There are two elementals at the heart of the city, far older than the one you have hidden in your house. Oh, you thought I didn't know?" She laughed, a rich, lilting sound that didn't fit with the destruction around them. "Your willingness to exist at the edge of our empire wasn't the best method for being unseen, Vasa. I know that you intentionally sent your children to study with heads full of misinformation." She cocked her head, raising a finger as if a thought just occurred. "Tell me, did you have children just so you could use them like tools? Is that why you're going to let Keiron die, so that you may usurp our power and install yourselves as some kind of royal family? The ones that live, of course. Who *knows* what might be happening to your family right now, especially since it seems that law and order has left our ranks." She looked mournfully out at the echoes of destruction left behind by the mass exodus of angels. Their collective fear left wreckage of every kind behind, including the dead, and some who would soon join them.

"I ask you to step aside, Utipa. There's no need for further bloodshed today." Saiinov's hand slipped to the hilt of his sword. Habira mirrored his action. Both looked willing to kill once more, if it came to that.

Her short bark of laughter rang into the lingering uproar. "Do you think you were the first angels to find evidence of something other than our empire?"

Saiinov said nothing. Habira looked confused, but Vasa lifted a brow, curious. It was a knowing look, hinting at even more secrets.

"I know you've been collecting ancient shells covered in script no one can read. Maybe no one except for you, Vasa." Utipa smiled, one professional to another. "Our people didn't always exist, and neither did this empire. Or Sliver, or the houses floating serenely above something so unknown that we're trained not even to think about what might be lurking underneath our delicate feet. It's a hard world that we live in, but we do quite well. We shape the wind, and storms, and we hunt and kill beasts that are the stuff of nightmares. Oh, we lose a few people here and there, but nothing that would make us think we cannot continue to survive as a race." She drew a breath that was something less than a shudder, but still brimming with barely contained fear. "You've set your power play into motion, but it isn't going to end here, not even close. Do you know *where* we came from? Do you understand why so many of the beasts that ply the skies around us look as if they were meant to live in the water of a storm? Don't you find that curious in the least?" She had them now. Her questions were excellent, and not unique within the walls of their house.

"I don't know, but I have my suspicions," Vasa said, her tone neutral.

A guard screamed as he was dragged down from a parapet by a triad of angels, their armor all red and green. It was a minor house, but they were rising up to kill within the walls of Sliver. The rebellion was at hand, and safety was no longer guaranteed for anyone. Not with the council in retreat, and House Windhook with only a handful of wounded to stem the tide of anarchy. "Some of the animals are stranger still, having no wings at all."

"That is strange, isn't it? It's almost as if they came from the land, but that would be impossible since we tell our children that there *is* no land beneath us, only roiling fire and death." Some of Utipa's playful nature returned with her questions. Her eyes darted about as the noise level began to increase. There were more red and green shapes flying about, met in the air by a house whose only color was a soft blue. The roar of wings began to beat the air as three more houses made their move in an attempt to seize control while the situation was still fluid. Angels flew with swords extended, slicing indiscriminately at anything that didn't wear the armor of their house. Cries of agony marked successful strikes as winners and losers emerged in the shifting masses of flying warriors.

"You've overstayed your welcome, Windhook. You might die here with me if we don't leave, and even then it will be a close thing, I think." Utipa bunched her leg muscles, preparing to take off vertically through the bloodshed.

"Will you join us?" Saiinov's question cut the momentary lapse of words like an icy rain.

"And do what? Die here? Fight and retreat only to come back into—all this?" Utipa was stunned at their arrogance, but then she let a sly smile quirk her lips. She was underestimating Windhook. Again.

Shadows flowed across the destruction of The Grievance as Airdancers began to descend, their flanks a hypnotic ripple of light and motion. The beasts were huge, wide, and flat but graceful to the point of delicacy, blocking out large swaths of sun and sky as they began to rotate downward in a spiral. There were six in all, and upon four of them rode the daughters of House Windhook, triumphant in their stirrups. The growing power of their house was apparent in the sheer extravagance of winged beings riding beasts. Their intent was clear; their ability even more so.

"Father! We brought friends!" Prista called down from her enormous mount, its flanks glowing in the weakening late sun. The Airdancers were a chatty bunch, flashing messages to and fro with a dizzying array of light in a language known only to them. Their delta wings rolled up and down smoothly, bringing them ever closer to the dais in a flowing mass of color and lights that verged in and out of the visible spectrum. Airdancers were alternately vivid or shadowed, but always elegant in their motions. To ride them was a mark of trust and skill, traits shared by almost all of the Windhook children.

Slender, dark, and intense, Banu and Vesta rode a pair of slightly smaller Airdancers that matched the twins well. The Watershapers of the family rode with their hands free, ready to invoke powerful magic on any and all water vapor within Sliver. Their abilities were serious, just as their matching dark blue eyes, which surveyed the scene with dispassionate professionalism. They were young, but incredibly skilled, and their beasts rode in a tightly controlled circle round The Grievance, dipping slightly to allow them better vision over the fleeing masses.

Prista's blonde hair was pulled back to give her full view of the scene as well, her Scholar's robe fluttering in waves as she continued her descent. Her hazel eyes burned with intellect in a face that marked her as Saiinov's child; she had features that were angular, pretty, and strong. "I trust we'll be in time? It would appear that Sliver is about to undergo a change of government." She grinned broadly before seeing the extent of her mother's wounds. "Is she —" Her voice faltered, shocked at Vasa's appearance. "Mother? Can you fly?"

"With these? No. On your mount? Yes." Vasa coughed and tucked her wings behind her in a flurry of frustration. She was a proud woman, and unused to any sort of incapacitation, especially at the hands of something other than childbirth. With her lips pressed in a pale line, she moved to Prista, who lifted her in conjunction with Saiinov's strong, practiced grip. Their gentle motion and regard spoke to the severity of her wounds, despite her unwillingness to admit them.

"I think our die is cast, love." Saiinov's rumble in his wife's ear was meant to reassure, but it only led to mild alarm. They had clearly reached a point in their plans where things became less defined, and more susceptible to the laws of chaos. At her rounded eyes and sheen of sweat, he knew their next stop must be at the port, where they would collect their vessel and prepare for a fighting retreat. The Airdancers were worth their weight in glyphs at that point, giving the family a collective menace that made their safe departure just a bit more likely. They would need it. Not everyone would regard House Windhook as liberators.

As one, the Airdancers began to ascend in a controlled, fluid arc, taking the family that sparked a rebellion into the sky and circling outward to the long curve of the city docks. As they approached, Saiinov shouted over the commotion, "Look! They're scattering!"

He was right. Windships of every imaginable size were falling, rising, and fleeing like hunted beasts, throwing lines off in hurried distress as their families and crew tried to leave the carnage of Sliver. Angels were brave and strong, but it was better to retreat to the safety of one's House than fight an unknown enemy for a cause that was still in its infancy. They would flee, and then, when the clouds had calmed and cooler heads prevailed, they would scheme and rally and return. Saiinov intended to have his family long gone by that time, safely ensconced in the protective walls of Windhook, their elemental watching a vigil over them as they healed and prepared for the actual war.

Vasa slipped in an out of consciousness as her children took turns moving her from the rippling back of the Airdancer directly onto the deck of their ship. Had she been even a little stronger, she could have ridden the elegant beast all the way to their home, safe on its broad back and surrounded by its littermates in a lethal cocoon of graceful fury.

The bitter cry behind them was followed by a bolt of withering energy that struck Vasa'a Airdancer deep in its exposed flank. Wild with pain, the animal twisted to hurl her over the side of the windship, saved only by her hand, which wrapped painfully in a dangling line. Instantly, her body weight began to tighten the silken rope into a lethal cutting force, causing her fingers to blanch into a ghostly shade of white.

"Traitorous filth!" Factor Sibilla stood bleeding less than twenty feet away on the swaying length of the dock. Clearly, the rebellion had not been kind to her in its first moments; she was missing a great section of one wing, and there was a long wound down her cadaverous cheek. She spat wind herbs at them and began to muster another glyph of power, her small black eyes fairly pulsing with hatred at the family that ended her life of power and privilege. She was bony, and vile, and crooked in ways that spoke of a mind that was concerned only with pain and hatred. In her twisted face, there was nothing of reason or justice, only a mindless desire to cause hurt in the last moments of her life. She giggled, a girlish noise of wanton joy, savoring the agony on Vasa's face as she twisted in the rising winds.

"It hurts, doesn't it? Knowing that your fall is so close?" Sibilla's voice was more normal now, although there was a rattle in her lungs that sounded like the end of an era. "You won't win cleanly, not even with all your plans." Her pale hands raised to deliver another masterful spell, the origin unknown but doubtless intended to kill.

Habira looked at her sword thoughtfully. With a shrug, she threw it, end over end, watching with satisfaction as the heavy pommel thumped into Sibilla's ribs. Her strike was far from deadly; in fact, it was little more than an inconvenience to the ancient Factor, but it was a distraction, and that was all she needed. Banu and Vesta leapt from their mounts to seize the hateful Scholar with the grip of youth and conviction, lifting her up to struggle helplessly as Prista dismounted and walked calmly forward, a length of hide in her hands. She regarded the spitting, hissing angel with something between pity and shame, then wrapped the hide tightly around Sibilla's wings, binding them together with an expert series of knots that left no room for motion or argument.

"You wanted to control the skies," said Prista, her voice a soft coo of delight, "and now, you shall." She nodded as the twins hurled the writhing creature over the side of the docks, screaming in frustration as she descended into the undulating clouds of the storm below the city. Sibilla did not fall far, as her body was seized by the grasping tendrils of an enormous colony of wind herbs, their thorns sinking into her flesh and beginning to greedily suck the rich nutrients from her body. Harvesting wind herbs was dangerous work; but being harvested by their predatory vines was the ultimate insult. In seconds, the thing that had been Factor Sibilla was a husk held together only by armor and echoes of hatred, and then the plant dropped it to fall through the clouds, lost forever.

Saiinov pulled his wife aboard, her hand a swollen, pale mass. She fought tears, gasping in pain as the family rallied around her, cutting the bound line away to free the woman who had given them life, and a home, and their collective wisdom. "Are you all right, love?" His words were tender, but hopeful.

Through a mix of joy and pain, Vasa smiled. "Take us home."

Saiinov nodded at his children, who cut the remaining lines and put the ship in motion, and it creaked to life under the power of winds that brought change and uncertainty to the empire of the skies. House Windhook would be at the center of all things for the near future and beyond, if they had their way. Grimly, they busied themselves trimming the ship for speed as Saiinov tended his wife.

There was much to be done, and sky enough for all of it.

CHAPTER SEVENTEEN:

The Fall

*L*iv! You've *got* to help." Dozer was in a state that Livvy found nothing short of surreal. Dozer didn't lose his cool. Ever. And yet, here he was, panting like he'd run a race, hair disheveled and looking about with eyes that flickered with animal wariness.

"What is it?" Livvy found herself wanting to whisper, wondering if there was a wild beast loose in the library. Stranger things had happened, according to Drum Circle Danny, but she was almost certain he'd been lying about the deer and its alleged rampage through the first floor copy room.

"Henatis." One word, but he loaded it with all of the menace that one might address an oncoming army of marauders. "I screwed up. I *really* — "

"Calm down." A chill of utter competence rushed over Livvy. She wasn't afraid of *Terezza* and her tomb-like office filled with — well, any number of things that creeped her out, not the least of which was a table that resembled a fog bank with an attitude. Still, Dozer was her rock. She could be his, at least this once. "Stop fidgeting. You're making it worse. Look at me. That's better. Okay, what do we need to do? I assume you pierced the inner sanctum and, what, dropped her favorite battle axe or something else she uses for fun on weekends?" She tried a little levity, but it fell with a thud.

His eyes were still brimming with something that was a bit too close to fear for her tastes. "Worse. I. . . ." He hesitated, waving long fingers in a motion that could have been anything from sign language to a rude gesture in a distant country. "You just have to see. Seriously, I'm done. So. Done."

Livvy stood, smoothing her pants with hands that went clammy with excitement. This was a chance to be like someone other than herself. It was too good to pass up, and no matter what, Dozer had been in her corner. She thought about how he roasted Britney and her crew, and decided that for him, once more into the breach and all that was just fine—even if it was the office of a woman who might secretly own a necklace made out of doll's ears or some-thing else suitably nefarious. "Come on. Show me." She gestured to him with her most haughty wave, turning for the door to Miss Henatis' office without a second glance.

They were going in.

The second floor was deserted, and for once Livvy was thankful not to see her regulars. They stopped before the plain door with the bronze name plate, feeling a low hum of anticipation as she turned the handle and opened it to a room that was dark and still. "Are you sure you were in here? There isn't a fire, or an ongoing lava flow. What did you do?"

The light flicked on as Dozer closed the door point-edly, revealing a crowd of people looking at her with a range of emotions. Danny looked sad, while Miss Willie wouldn't look at her at all. Dozer's face was closed off, resigned to something unpleasant in a way that Livvy had seen so many times before when a doctor was getting ready to make her scream with pain.

But it was Frank, the vendor from the plaza, who confused her. He slapped his hands together in the quiet moment, his expression one of acceptance at a task that he could neither escape nor condone. Livvy knew all of the expressions around her, and she began to weakly force air into to her lungs for what she knew would be the last scream of her life.

"I told you she wouldn't go quietly. They never do." Miss Henatis stood next to her unusual table, its mist crawling up and out of the glass edges with a hungry fervor that was repulsive and graceful. With a rueful shrug, she looked at Frank. "Muffle her. I've had enough of this one for one lifetime."

An iron hand clamped around Livvy's mouth as she was lifted, kicking and shrieking into the painfully dead air that filled her throat. Spots began to form as her eyes implored Dozer with a plea — *save me. Save me! Why aren't you helping?*

He did nothing, merely stepping past her to lift the shining glass lid of the table, now pulsing with iron-colored light that was hopeless and menacing all at once. "I told you I was your best friend, and I meant it. I know that means nothing right now, but you have to believe me. You *must* stop fighting. This is happening, kid, and it's going to make sense someday if you live, just not right now."

The lid was thrown back as the mist reached for her in shapeless fingers of dread. Dozer's eyes filled with tears, but then he did something that made Livvy sick with loss. He smiled, put his hand on the back of her head, and pushed her into the yawning space filled with mist — and then nothing.

Finally, she screamed, but there was no one around to hear it, and the world was gone forever. She began to fall and never stopped, not even when her tears were the only thing left that she knew was real. For a moment, she thought that her tears would make the world beautiful, like a broken mirror if there was only enough light for her to see them, but there was no light in the place she fell.

She knew that her hope, like Dozer's friendship, was a lie.

CHAPTER EIGHTEEN:

Livvy

*R*ed lights flashed in pulsating arcs as sirens began winding down, their cries fading, only to be replaced by a flurry of shouts and commands. Shoes slapped the concrete in every direction as the ambulances began to disgorge their cargo of victims, some howling in pain, others fearfully quiet. Some people ran, and some walked quickly, their faces a mask of intense concentration. The stink of gas fumes, blood, and fear hung in the air over a layer of diesel fumes that was trapped under the alcove of the hospital emergency entrance. It was a humid summer night, and there were no stars, only the dull orange glow of a city pushing against the sky overhead, keeping the globe of sullen light just out of reach of the people below. There were secrets to be had, but not for the city. Then the stars winked for a bare moment, letting everyone in on the joke before vanishing behind banks of clouds that broke apart from indecision in the building breeze. Rain was coming, and soon.

One ambulance swung wide before lurching to a halt,

only to be followed by four more, rocking on their springs as they crowded the emergency lane like cattle at a trough. The roaring engines blatted against concrete walls before dying as one, turned off to allow the frantic staff to pry their cargo free on the wheeled gurneys, rattling with harried motion and the calls of *one, two, three, lift* over and over. Livvy heard the shouts, knowing that she should understand something, but wondering why her ears were ringing so badly. There was noise — jagged, brutal noise — no, a pain made into sound — ringing throughout her head in an endless loop, punishing her senses without mercy. A face hovered over her, shining a light into one eye, then the next. She tried to speak, but couldn't. There was no wind, and a sputtering cough was all she could manage as the fumes from the ambulances crawled into her nose and lungs with each frantic gasp.

"She's conscious," came the male voice. It was urgent, even fevered.

She couldn't see who it was, and her head — why wouldn't her head move? She tried to flex her neck, but it was locked in place by something firm on either side, like blocks. More voices began to shout as the telltale ratcheting of metal gurneys filled Livvy's hearing. She heard a moan, then a scream cutting through the chaos as someone was moved, their pleading cry for a mother or something distorting into a formless gurgle that sent chills dancing over her skin. It was a noise of agony so distilled that Livvy winced in sympathy despite her own body being awash in pain.

A doctor — nurse — a person, she knew that, and not much more as the form leaned when the doors slid open to admit them into the austere bustle of the emergency room.

The wheels of her stretcher rolled smoothly over the floor as lights began to flicker past in pairs like long, sterile blurs on a highway at night. If anything, the noise increased as Livvy felt herself being turned into a wide room with brilliant, painful light and the chemical scents of disinfect- ant and stiff linen. It was thronged with people in surgical scrubs. One of them put a stethoscope to her bare chest; it was a frigid shock that made her nearly cry out, but she had neither the breath nor the strength to protest.

"I know, honey, it's really cold. At least you're here to feel it." The voice was busy but warm. It was a woman, and she sounded like a friend.

"Am I home?" Livvy croaked. It was little more than a whisper.

"Shhh. We're going to take good care of you and your friends, honey. What's your name?" Busy fingers were cutting away her clothing. Livvy felt a flash of shame.

"Livvy Foster." It was all she could manage.

"That's what I thought." The nurse turned away and began speaking in a rapid-fire voice that she'd clearly used before. There were responses that Livvy couldn't discern, then the nurse said, "He's here? Good. Tell him we'll have her ready. Doctor, is she good to go?" The words were competent, the questions asked to seek confirmation rather than something unknown.

A new set of hands began examining her with cool professionalism. He said not a word, but examined her chest, her arms, and finally, a throbbing pain in her ankle that she only noticed when he touched it. Pain lanced upward, then died away in a flash. "She's got superficial bruising. How the kid made it, I have no idea, but we have to go now." There was amazement in his voice, and a hint of uncertainty. Something was going to happen, and he didn't want it. Not yet, anyway.

"Are you sure? She's — look at her. Those scars? She's had multiple surgeries." The female nurse was openly dubious.

"I know, and she's on the list. She hit the lottery twice in one night, and if we're going to save her, it happens now or not at all." He turned away to a new presence.

"I'm glad I left the boat in its slip this weekend. Had a feeling we might be needed. Someone called for a glorified plumber?" It was a man, his voice deep, comforting, with a personable accent that radiated competence.

"Sailor Mark. The one time you don't go out on the water, and here she is." The first doctor laughed, then took Livvy's hand. "We're going to prep you for surgery right now, and I have to do some things that might be unpleasant. No, don't try to speak. Your parents are on their way, and we're doing everything we can to save the girls who hit you. Their vehicle rolled, and all of them have head trauma, but they're young, and healthy, and we have every doctor in the city here right now. One of them asked about you — Britney is her name, I think, so you rest easy, okay? I'm going to intubate you, and when you wake up you're going to have a new heart, Livvy." When tears began to stream down her face, he got closer, wiping them away. The nurse took her other hand as he smiled. "Do you know what that means? Intubate? I'm going to put a tube down your throat to help you breathe. Usually we'd give you anesthetic, but we don't have time because of the transplant."

"Transplant?" Livvy mouthed.

"Your heart is here. The donor is — your heart is here, Livvy, and we have to move quickly. Dr. Marks and the whole team are going to make certain you get the through this, okay? But right now, this is going to be unpleasant, and I'm sorry, but we're out of time." He looked away, nodding. "We'll begin right now. Nurse Williams, get the other team around." His face came into focus as he blocked the lights, and the smile was so warm and assuring that she felt herself begin to relax despite all of the fear and pain. "I'm very good at this, Livvy, so from this moment on, you can consider me your best friend. I promise, I'll do everything I can to make this as quick and easy as I can. It might feel like a bulldozer, but it'll be over soon."

"That's how he got his nickname. The Dozer." Nurse Willie laughed, shaking her head. "You're in the best hands, honey. Dr. Dozier is going to save you." There was a pause, then the nurse they called Willie added, "We all are."

"Is Dr. Daniels ready with anesthesia?" came another voice.

It was Dr. Marks. She smiled. She knew that voice. Her pain began to fade. She was meant to be there, in that moment.

"Ready to keep the beat. Let's go." The man she knew as Danny looked down at her with a gentle smile. "You'll go to sleep, and when you wake up, I'll make sure it's my face you see first, not his." He jerked his head at Dozer with a smirk. "He isn't nearly as handsome as I am. Wouldn't want to scare your new heart." He winked theatrically, and Livvy's face bloomed in a smile of joyous relief. The swirl of emotions cascaded over her, drowning her fear one gentle touch at a time.

"Counting back from ten, now," Dr. Daniels said, his voice calm and professional.

Dozer touched her shoulder, his smile fading to an

expression of intense concentration.

"All together on this one, people. She's come a long way for this." It was Dozer, and those were the last words Livvy heard before her eyes closed and the darkness came rushing up once again.

CHAPTER NINETEEN:

Heartborn

$\mathcal{W}$aking was easy. Staying that way was hard.

Livvy's eyes fluttered daintily until she muttered a soft grunt of anger and kept her eyes open with a steely effort. The room was clean and bland, like all hospitals, but there were splashes of color swimming in her eyes. They seemed to shout among the tan and soft gray around her, loud and alive.

"Flowers." One word was all she managed before someone slipped a straw into her mouth. It was water, cold and heavenly. She thought about crying, and it might have been from the water, or the lingering pain, or something else she couldn't describe. Livvy's throat worked and she spoke again, lifting her head with the delicacy of a bomb technician at work. "Mom? Dad?"

There was no answer, just a rustling of sorts as someone came closer. "They're getting more coffee, honey. I think their veins must be nothing but caffeine sludge at this point." There was a low chuckle as blankets were drawn back up over her. "They've been awake for more than a day, and I've never seen two people look more like a pair of owls watching you, waiting for your eyes to open. Your parents love you more than all the waves on the ocean, you know."

At that, Livvy reached out, wanting human contact and reassurance. Her vision began to clear, suddenly, as a sense of well-being trickled into her with each passing breath. There was something new, but it danced outside her understanding. The feeling was not hers to know. Not yet.

It was Miss Willie who took her hand with a grip that was warm and strong. Her dark eyes were glimmering with tears, but she was smiling. It was a look of such joyous abandon that Livvy felt a wave of confusion. She hadn't died, or at least she didn't feel that way. After another experimental breath, she was certain of it, and she sincerely hoped that if she made it to heaven the décor would be a bit fancier. "I'm fine, Miss Willie. You saw to it." When Livvy's eyes cleared, she saw a face regarding her with such intense concern, she wondered if the surgery had gone wrong in some new and terrible way. They hovered apart in the moment, not out of fear for contact, but so that they could look at each other. There was something unsaid behind Miss Willie's tears. It took her three tries to speak to the patient, who was so much more than that.

"I've been with you since your first surgery. Did you know that?" The voice was not that of a nurse, but something more. Like family.

"I — no, I didn't. Thank you?" It seemed pitifully inadequate.

Miss Willie smiled as the tears faded. Her features took on a look of conspiracy, and then simple glee. "We always knew that you weren't ours to have. Oh, Liv." She laughed, a rich, warm sound of relief and pride. "How I have waited through these years to see this. You're everything I hoped for and more."

"You knew? How?" Livvy was pained by confusion. How could Miss Willie have known the truth if she was a woman of earth? Of this time? The pieces clashed. There was no sense to it, even in a world where time could move backward and people could cheat death.

Miss Willie looked upward, seeing nothing. In the light, Livvy noticed that her eyes had the most amazing flecks of gold in their rich darkness, like beacons of wisdom. "Some of us can see both places, and we knew. We've always known the truth of you, Livvy. And Keiron. Even the trials ahead of you — and they are many, I tell you, but you'll rise to the challenge. I've always felt it, even when the future is a murk of war and deceit. But in here" — she patted Livvy's chest, gently — "You have everything needed to lead. To win. You were born for this, girl, and now the only thing left is to tell the people you love, and one more small detail."

"Which is?" Livvy was dumbfounded. The Seers were real, and Miss Willie was one of them. She looked at her friend through eyes filled with respect, and maybe a little awe.

"You're going to need a Lieutenant, but I don't think you'll have a hard time finding one."

Cressa stepped from the shadows, a slender form clad only in scrubs. They hung on her like someone else's clothes, and she pulled at the collar with an impatient, childish tug. "I was too late, Livvy. Can you forgive me?"

"Too late? For what?" Alarm began to build like an

oncoming storm, before slapping her with a cold reality that made her stomach vault into a sickening knot. "Where—" she began, but she knew. The words were like lumps of cold ash on her tongue, dead and gray. With hot tears rolling freely, Livvy uttered the question like a priest calling to the rafters of an empty church. The answer was known; the words, meaningless. The only thing that mattered was the weight of the truth, crushing her without mercy as she lay in a sterile bed with her heart pumping away in perfect rhythm. "Where's Keiron? Where *is* he?"

The heart monitor gave an angry chirp and began to speed up, powered into a gallop by the horrible realization that Keiron was, in fact, in the room. But not all of him.

Livvy touched her chest, trying hard to forgive her own flawed, broken body part that had once been, but was gone. "Who are you?" Through an ocean of pain, the question was launched to pierce Cressa, who stood watching the scene with her hands clenched into knots of regret.

Cressa knelt awkwardly beside the bed, fearful of touching Livvy lest she come apart from sheer grief. "I'm sorry." She didn't know what else to say, so her name would have to do. "Cressa. I—I know about you, and Keiron. I thought I would be able to help them fight, but I was told to jump, to sacrifice myself. For you . . . and Keiron. I don't think I'm supposed to be alive, not really. I think that was the plan, and I screwed up because I didn't know where I was going. I jumped." The last words were uttered in shameful amazement.

Livvy looked at her in disbelief. "You jumped? From where?"

Miss Willie moved to the bed, leaning in slightly like

mother wolf. "Don't worry about that, Liv. You've got a lot of healing to do, and there'll be time for talking later on. You must rest. Your heart cannot be stressed, not now."

"You mean Keiron's heart, right?" The accusation was weakened by a dull pain that swept through Livvy like guilty lightning. She was too weak to fight, and too desperate to survive. It sickened her that she was bound to such desires, because at that second she wanted nothing more than to vanish from the face of the earth and send the heart beating in her chest back to its rightful owner

"Yes, Keiron's," Livvy's dad said with conflicted joy. Her parents stood in shock for the briefest of seconds, like deer momentarily blinded by headlights. Then time began to click forward once more, and they rushed to the bed and held Livvy's hands with a kind of hopeful delicacy that hinted at so much more waiting under the surface. There was a cloud of fearful joy around them as they began to speak in staccato sentences of giddy, meaningless phrases. Their daughter was alive. She had a heart — a good one — and now she could begin the long, painful slog toward healing that lay ahead.

After enough time to let the commotion fade into a general air of exhausted happiness, Miss Willie spoke once again, but this time there was authority in her words.

"Livvy, I think you should listen to Cressa. She's come a long way to find you, and if it weren't for the fickle nature of time, it might be her heart beating in your chest, unless I'm wrong." She cocked a brow at Cressa, who nodded with dull admission.

"Why? How?" Livvy's voice shook with uncertainty.

Cressa looked down, her cheeks blazing with shame. "I said I was too late."

"I got that the first time," Livvy snapped, then covered her mouth in apology. "Sorry. I'm just — this is a lot to take in." Tears rolled down her cheeks, with no end in sight.

With a sigh of acceptance, Cressa began kneading her fingers together, looking for all the world like a nervous child. After closing her eyes, she finally began to speak. The air in the room grew still at the first quavering notes of her voice, but she gained momentum in a matter of seconds as the enormity of her location began to sink in.

"I followed Keiron because I thought it was the only way to save him, and his people. His family told me as much, and at first I didn't know, but then — " She hesitated, face twisting with the admission of something that had been buried. "I thought I could save myself, too."

"*His* people?" Livvy asked pointedly. "Aren't they your people as well? Who are you, Cressa?" The last of her question was soft, almost gentle. She could see the girl was in pain, and felt like she was under attack. Livvy knew that look, and empathized.

"My people, then. But not really, because I was no one. I was invisible to most, reviled by many. I was a thing, not a person, called a Blightwing. My colors told the world the only thing they would care about. I was a murderer. I *am* a murderer." She was on the verge of breaking down as memories overwhelmed her. Cressa's journey began before she chose to pierce the light of days; in actuality, it started the second she fought back against her treacherous sister. With some effort, she inhaled, then snapped her eyes to Livvy, who watched her with frank interest. "Do you understand, Livvy? I looked like them, but I wasn't one of them. Not really."

Livvy looked down at her chest, which was hidden by

bandages. "I do." She motioned to Cressa that she should come closer.

After a hesitant second, she did, and she stood awkwardly midway down the left side of the enormously complex bed.

Livvy took her hand with a careful grip, letting them get used to the idea that they were both real and in the same room. "I'm seventeen years old, and nearly every second of my life has been in the skin of a girl who didn't belong, and not because of who I was, but something I was missing. Were you missing anything?" The question was rhetorical. Cressa stared at their hands, clasped lightly together. Livvy tried to smile, but failed. Rather, her face was filled with understanding. "I think you were. Maybe you needed someone to defend you? Is that why you became a killer?"

A single tear fell from Cressa's eye, leaving only a shining track in the harsh light of the room. It was an admission of loneliness that Livvy knew as a constant companion in her own life. "I would have liked that, but it wasn't meant to be." She shrugged in defeat. "There was nothing for me except an act of sacrifice, and I couldn't even get that right. And yes, I needed someone to — just to help, but I didn't have it. So I became foul. A killer."

"I don't think you liked it. The killing. And you're here now, and that's good enough for me." Livvy forced herself to speak the words that would forgive a girl who was miles and years away from home, if such a place even existed anymore. She suspected it didn't, which meant that this girl, crying and alone, was in need of a friend. She'd have to think on the rest of it, because the ache in her chest wasn't just from the surgeon's cut. It was for Keiron, and the waste of it all, and knowing that the world was *much* different than she'd ever imagined. But it was Keiron who drew her thoughts into a whirling mass of shadows and light, joy and pain. His mind, and his smile, and the things he could have done. Gone. Sacrificed, and not by a girl who was brave enough to take the ultimate risk to give herself to the fates, but by something evil, maybe, or at the very least unknown. Livvy let the tiles fall into place, placing thoughts and conversations with Keiron side by side until she was ready to ask a question that floated into her thoughts like an unwelcome guest.

"Mom, Dad? Did you know about the Crescent Council?"

They didn't hesitate, for their policy with Livvy had been founded on two simple principles: truth and love. Both nodded, waiting. They knew that there was more to be told.

"I heard someone say Heartborn. What is that? There's no sense in holding anything back, I'm already well past my ration of weird for one lifetime." Livvy looked surprised at her own words, adding, "Sorry, Miss Willie. No offense to your whole ability to look into other realms, or whatever you call it."

"None taken, dear. I like to think of myself as a sentinel, looking out for a very specific kind of, ah, person. You are too, you know, although you've been terribly preoccupied for most of your life. That ended yesterday." Miss Willie regarded Livvy with a warmth that was nearly reverent. She knew what Livvy was. What she would be.

Livvy looked alarmed, inviting everyone in the room save Cressa to ask what was the matter. When the minor uproar collapsed out of necessity, she asked a question in a small voice, quite different than her earlier curiosity. She was hesitant, eyes darting slightly to take in details.

"Is this real?"

In answer, her mother leaned over her with a delicacy like no other and kissed her on the forehead. "It's real, Liv. You are here, with us, just as you should be." She sighed, a short, conflicted noise that her daughter had never heard before. After a brief look upward, eyes unfocused, she returned her attention to Livvy and began stroking her hair. "There are so many things for you to know. So many decisions."

"Why do I feel like the decisions aren't really mine?" Livvy asked, darkly. Reality was being imposed over the sense of awe at finding her world to be more complicated than she'd ever imagined.

Her dad broke in, urgent with the truth. "Honey, they are. All of your life is yours, with the exception of one thing. You had to have a heart. Do you know what the doctors told us the day you were born?" His face was stricken with memory as his mind took him someplace he'd closed off long ago. "Don't bother naming her. She won't be here long." He shook his head, and there was an old pain in his eyes that made Livvy want to leave the bed and hug him.

Her mother's eyes were moist with tears, and Miss Willie couldn't even look at her.

"Were you there?" Livvy's question was part accusation, which she instantly regretted.

"I was." Miss Willie's nod was slow, deliberate. "But then I held you. We all did, if only for a second. It was Dozer who told your mother to pick out a name. I didn't know who he was, not then, but over time I came to know the truth. Your parents were first, because ultimately the truth was a family issue. Heartborn, they told us. I'd seen — I'd seen things, but unfocused, and fragmented. My life had been a torment, Livvy. I had vision without context, but then you came along. That all changed, and I knew that my life's work was seeing you to adulthood. To see you with another heart, and a life. And maybe, just maybe, you could do the things I saw."

There was silence in the room, broken only by a light mechanical noise of unknown origin. It was a complicated thing to keep a transplant patient stable, and the room was full with people and tools.

And curiosity.

"What did you see?" Livvy's voice returned in full, without a hint of the warble that she'd lived with for so long.

"Do you want to tell her, Cressa? You may as well. You're going to be there." Miss Willie smiled at the girl who had gone silent, standing next to the bed in a cloud of uncertainty.

Cressa rubbed her palms on her thighs as she formed the words. When she finally looked at Livvy, a half smile played at her lips, and for the first time she looked genuinely happy.

"Well, you're going to need a sword."

EPILOGUE:

They buried Keiron under an Ash tree that covered his grave like a protective mother dog. He looked small, wrapped in a snow white sheet. At the last, Livvy's father covered his face, placing two small, round stones on his eyes. He'd painted the stones silver and blue, letting them dry in the sun as he dug the grave with the help of Miss Willie, who cried without shame as she worked. Livvy felt her heart beat in time with their shovels. She cried herself dry by the time the hole was deep enough, and they lowered Keiron slowly down. Inside Livvy, there was a spreading numbness spiked with random pains.

I am with you.

Livvy looked around, thinking to ask if anyone else had heard, but their faces indicated nothing of the sort. Wind rose around them, rustling through the trees before moving on. A lightness grew deep within her, from feet to heart to her shoulders as Keiron did what he could to ease her pain. She was thankful for the relief, and hoping that he was not hurting, wherever he was. She didn't think so, but if anyone had asked, she couldn't have given anything resembling a reason. "Won't people ask questions?" Livvy wondered how they had gotten Keiron here, and why no one seemed afraid of being accused of a crime.

After a long silence, her mother spoke. "In a thousand years, it won't matter." She would say nothing else, nor would anyone. It seemed that Keiron was destined to rest in solitude and shade, and that was that.

Fear began to gnaw at Livvy, who had been consumed with the grief of her pain, as well as a maelstrom of fearful questions, right up until the moment Keiron's echo spoke to her. Among these lingering doubts, one thing sat heaviest on her tongue. She had to ask.

"You're certain I can come back?" For Livvy, everything hinged on this simple question. She stood in her backyard, looking at the pond where she'd spent hours reading at an old iron bench. Water rippled over stones as her dad's goldfish lazed about, content with their lot in life. The pond was a perfect circle, hidden by their fence and partially covered by well-tended shrubs and flowers that occupied her mother during the warm afternoons when the entire family had unplugged from life to the retreat of their secret garden.

"Positive." It was a single word from her father, who looked as if he was going to implode from worry and pain. His face was streaked with dirt and sweat stung his eyes, but he'd been crying anyway so it didn't seem to matter. Her mother was doing a bit better, wearing an expression that wavered between pride and the verge of tears; in the stippled sunlight, she looked young and uncertain. A few minutes earlier, she had been a woman watching the burial of a child, which is the single most tragic thing that a mother can endure. The fact that Keiron was not her own didn't matter. Mothers know. And they always feel it, right down to their bones.

Livvy's throat was dry and tight, but above all else, she believed in their love. Keiron's heart — *her heart*, she corrected—thumped away in her chest without fail. Her lungs were filled with endless breath, and she'd never felt better in her entire life. Around her legs swirled a plain dress of white that Cressa had given her; where it came from, Livvy had no idea, but the fabric was nearly weightless, just like the long sword that rested in her palm. The blade fairly sang when she waved it, stirring ancient memories in her that made it seem like nothing more than an extension of her own hand. On her wrists were small bracers, another gift of Cressa that had an alien vibrancy to them, snugging easily around her graceful wrists as if made for that very purpose. For some reason, Livvy knew they had been, and let it go at that. She wore calf-length boots, clinging to the long muscles of her legs, and stood wiggling her toes experimentally to seat them into the unfamiliar footwear. Those had been a gift of Miss Willie, who said in no uncertain terms that Livvy was not to take them off until they were soft and supple. With a nod of promise, she'd thanked Miss Willie, although she didn't really understand how or why she was to achieve such levels of comfort in boots that would be taken off at night, and preferably in a few hours. She chalked it up to the mass of unknown things that loomed ahead of her, kept at bay only by the loving assurances of people who had done nothing but protect her for the last seventeen years.

Her mom took a step and embraced Livvy fiercely. "You *will* come back." It was part prayer, part statement.

Cressa cleared her throat, looking embarrassed. "The day is getting on. Not here," she said, looking at the high sun, "but there. She is needed."

Livvy took Cressa's hand, giving it a squeeze that was far more adult and confident than she was feeling at that moment. "*We* are needed, you mean." Her smile took the sting away from the correction as Cressa blushed lightly. In one moment, Livvy was growing into a role she'd been made for, causing her parents to beam as one at their daughter. She'd need Cressa at her side for the days ahead, and although she could not know it, years. There was much to be done in the sky.

"We'll be here," said her dad, simply. There was nothing else to say. She was Heartborn, and her calling lay before her, waiting to unspool in a mystery of power and danger. Livvy and Cressa stepped down into the pool, scattering the goldfish in darting flashes of orange panic. Where their boots touched, the water began to illuminate into whirlpools of luminous blue, swirling away with a sinuous grace until the light covered all, and the humble yard began to fade.

"Where will we go?" It seemed inadequate, but Livvy burned to know the exact location of her arrival.

"Center pool in House Windook. They'll be waiting, I imagine." Cressa waved at Livvy's parents, who stood bathed in the ethereal light of Livvy's destiny.

Their tears sparkled with gemlike light as the air grew brighter and their lips were moving and there was no sound—

Brightness, and wind. A smell of rain and the snapping of fabric in a large space. Livvy's eyes cleared as she took her first look at House Windhook, its delicate marine whorls surrounding her in a translucent catacomb of grace and power.

Saiinov and Vasa stood, dignified but hopeful. Their faces were regal in bearing. Vasa seemed to be hiding a smile, but Saiinov was openly appraising her. Livvy stood, pulling Cressa to her feet after a tumble upon their arrival in the utter dislocation of the pool.

Saiinov stuck out a hand in welcome, his dark eyes fixed on Livvy with all the questions that a man could ever have. A smile broke through like the sun, and he pulled her up and out of the pool. "Welcome, Livvy. We've been waiting."

Livvy staggered under the weight of her newfound wings. Somehow, she'd expected them, but the smile that lit her face was part child and all wonder. She flexed them in all their snowy glory before settling her newest acquisition with a sensible flick. Folded in, they fit tightly against her slender frame as if going home. *I hate heights. How am I going to fly? Maybe it's like falling.* Her thoughts raced as she put a hand to her heart, feeling the strength of it as an alien presence in her chest. *I have a lot of things to learn.*

The four of them stood as the wind broke into the inner house, rushing cool on their faces. A Windbeast shrieked, distant and alien, its plaintive cry piercing the delicacy of the house with animalistic menace.

Livvy closed her eyes, letting the sound reverberate in her heart. There would be time for thanks later. For now, she too had questions, and the first one was easy.

"Did you know he was going to die?" Livvy pierced Saiinov with her gaze, then shifted to Vasa without remorse. A great deal of their lives depended on the next few moments. If there was a whiff of dishonesty — well,

Livvy had wings. She could go anywhere, now.

"No. Not for certain, but it wasn't our decision." Vasa's voice was flat, numb. She was processing a loss and a rebirth all in one moment.

Saiinov said nothing.

"Who decided that he should die so that I may live?"

Silence stretched, filled only with the winds. After the pause became stale, Vasa answered again, and this time there was real pain. "Fate? A careless god?" Her face crumpled, powerless to change that which had changed her. "He was a perfect babe, but when he was born with his eyes open, I knew. We all knew." Her voice broke on the last word, the plaintive cry of a mother who sees that her gift is only temporary.

"I would have given my own heart to save him. No hesitation." Saiinov's anguish was so close it made Livvy step back ever so slightly, as if his pain could harm her, too, like a detonation of hurt brought on through memory.

"Did you send Cressa in hopes she would die?" Livvy asked. It was a cold question.

Cressa said nothing, but looked askance at Vasa. She had suspicions about the purity of the grieving mother and her motivations. She'd seen too much of the family to believe that they entered into any ploy without options, and those choices might mean the death of an innocent if it aided their cause.

"Yes." Vasa looked down at the empty sky. "I would do it again, too."

REVIEWS

If you enjoyed *Heartborn*, please consider leaving a rating and review on the site where you bought it. All genuine comments and feedback are welcome.

Reviews and feedback are extremely important to Terry Maggert, as well as other potential readers, and would be very much appreciated. Thank you.

Let's stay in touch through my website and mailing list. It's spam free, with signing events, free book alerts, and upcoming projects:

www.terrymaggert.com/get-the-newsletter.html

ABOUT THE AUTHOR

Left-handed. Father of an apparent nudist. Husband to a half-Norwegian. Herder of cats and dogs. Lover of pie. I write books. I've had an unhealthy fascination with dragons since the age of — well, for a while. Native Floridian. Current Tennessean. Location subject to change based on insurrection, upheaval, or availability of coffee. Nine books and counting, with no end in sight. You've been warned.

Currently, I live near Nashville, Tennessee, with the aforementioned wife, son, and herd, and, when I'm not writing, I teach history, grow wildly enthusiastic tomato plants, and restore my 1967 Mustang.

CONTACT TERRY MAGGERT

Author's Blog: terrymaggert.com

Additional Social Media:
Twitter: twitter.com/TerryMaggert
Facebook: facebook.com/terrymaggertbooks
Goodreads: goodreads.com/terry_maggert
Pinterest: pinterest.com/terry68
Amazon: amazon.com/Terry-Maggert/e/B00EKN8RHG/
Signed Paperbacks: Contact author directly via Facebook, or at terrymaggertbooks@gmail.com

MORE BOOKS BY TERRY MAGGERT

Halfway Bitten

The circus came to Halfway, and they brought the weird.

When clowns, vampires, and corpses start piling up in town, Carlie has to break away from her boyfriend, Wulfric, to bring her witchy skills to the table- or grill, as the case may be.

When the body of a young woman washes up in the lake, it unleashes a spiral of mystery that will bring Carlie, Gran, and Wulfric into a storm of magical warfare. Spells will fly. Curses will rain. Amidst it all, Carlie will make waffles, protect her town, and find out if a man from the distant past can join her in happy ever after.

With love and honor at stake, Carlie has no peer.

Halfway Dead

Carlie McEwan loves many things.

She loves being a witch. She loves her town of Halfway, NY—a tourist destination nestled on the shores of an Adirondack lake. Carlie loves her enormous familiar, Gus, who is twenty-five pounds of judgmental Maine Coon cat, and she positively worships her Grandmother, a witch of incredible power and wisdom. Carlie spends her days cooking at the finest — and only — real diner in town, and her life is a balance between magic and the mundane, just as she likes it.

When a blonde stranger sits at the diner counter and calls her by name, that balance is gone. Major Pickford asks Carlie to lead him into the deepest shadows of the forest to find a mythical circle of chestnut trees, thought lost forever to mankind. There are ghosts in the forest, and one of them cries out to Carlie across the years. Come find me.

Danger, like the shadowed pools of the forest, can run deep. The danger is real, but Carlie's magic is born of a pure spirit. With the help of Gus, and Gran, and a rugged cop who really does want to save the world, she'll fight to bring a ghost home, and deliver justice to a murderer who hides in the cool, mysterious green of a forest gone mad with magic.

Halfway Hunted

Some Prey Bites Back.

Welcome to Halfway; where the waffles are golden, the moon is silver, and magic is just around every corner.

A century old curse is broken, releasing Exit Wainwright, an innocent man trapped alone in time.

Lost and in danger, he enlists Carlie, Gran, and their magic to find the warlock who sentenced him to a hundred years of darkness. The hunter becomes the hunted when Carlie's spells awaken a cold-blooded killer intent on adding another pelt to their gruesome collection: hers.

But the killer has never been to Halfway before, where there are three unbreakable rules:

1. Don't complain about the diner's waffles.

2. Don't break the laws of magic.

3. Never threaten a witch on her home turf.

Can Carlie solve an ancient crime, defeat a ruthless killer and save the love of her life from a vampire's curse without burning the waffles?

Come hunt with Carlie, and answer the call of the wild.

Banshee

Cities Fall. Dragons Rise. War Begins.

The war for earth began in Hell. First came the earthquakes. Then came the floods. Finally, from the darkened mines, caves and pits, the creatures of our nightmares boiled forth to sweep across the planet in a wave of death.

On the run and unprepared, mankind is not alone. We have dragons.

Emerging from their slumber, giant dragons select riders to go to war. Their forces strike back at the legions of demons that attack on the night of every new moon. The Killing Moon, as it becomes known, is the proving ground for warriors of skill and heart. Among the riders is Saavin, a brave young woman from the shattered remains of Texas.

Her dragon, Banshee, is swift and fearless, but they will need help to fight a trio of monstrous creatures that Hell is using to take cities one by one.

With the help of French Heavener, a warrior of noble intent, Banshee and Saavin will launch a desperate defense of New Madrid, the last city standing. But first, they'll have to go into the very cave where demons bide their time until the sun fades and the moon is black.

The hope of mankind rests on dragon's wings and the bravery of Saavin and French.

They have the guts. They have the guns.

They have dragons.

The Forest Bull

Three lovers who stalk and kill the immortals that drift through South Florida (tourists are a moveable feast, after all) are living a simple life of leisure- until one of them is nearly killed by woman who is a new kind of lethal.

When Ring Hardigan isn't making sandwiches for, and with, his two partners, Waleska and Risa (they're cool like that), he's got a busy schedule doing the dirty work of sending immortals to the ever after. Wally and Risa provide linguistics, logistics, and finding the right place for him and his knife- together, they're a well-oiled machine, and they've settled into a rhythm that bodes ill for the Undying. Warlocks, vampires, succubae and the odd ghoul have all fallen to their teamwork. Life is tough, but they soldier on killing the undead, liberating their worldly goods for charity, and generally achieving very little.

Until Ring wakes up after nearly dying at the hands of a woman who may or may not be the daughter of Satan. Ring's a tough character, for a boat bum (killing immortals sort of rubs off on you that way), but twelve days of comatose healing are enough to bring out the ugly side of his temper. When a letter arrives asking for their help finding a large collection of stolen heirloom jewelry, they form an uneasy friendship with the last Baron of a family hiding in a primal European forest.

Cazimir, the Baron, has two skills: Jeweler and preserver of the last herd of forest bulls. It's an odd occupation, but then, Ring, Risa and Wally aren't your everyday career folks, and Cazimir's lodge might be sitting on something that looks a lot like hell, which, according to a 2400 year old succubus hooker named Delphine, is currently on the market to the strongest immortal. The Baron's impassioned plea to find the jewelry comes with some conditions- he doesn't want the collection back as much as he does the thief, Elizabeth, who happens to be his daughter- and the woman who nearly sent Ring to his grave.

In a tapestry of lies, it's up to Ring, Wally and Risa to find out what is evil, who is human, and exactly who really wants to reign over hell.

Mask of the Swan

Killing immortals is easy. Becoming one is hard.

When three lovers (Ring, Waleska, and Risa) take a vacation after losing a fight with an elegant monster named Elizabeth, their time for healing is cut short by a new threat, and this time, innocent blood will spill.

Reaching for the crown of Hell, Elizabeth gathers Archangels around her to fuel her power-mad ascent — but she has powerful enemies who will fight her every step of the way, including Delphine, the 2400 year old succubus hooker who knows that inside her beautiful body rests a very human soul. Joined by an honorable priest who finds himself in the middle of a war he never knew existed, a demigod and his partner, and the stage is set for another round in the battle to determine how much of Ring, Waleska, and Risa is still human, how tough their immortal side can be — and how far they are willing to go to protect the people they love from a creature who would burn their world to ashes.

The Waking Serpent

Evil is never still.

Something wicked is crossing the sea, a creature so old that none even remember its name — but it has not forgotten the taste of blood. With a succubus ally, a brave priest, and new friends who seem a little less human than most, The Fearless will meet the greatest challenge of their lives. An ancient adversary is stopping by to avenge a wrong from the depths of time in a fight to the death that will bring a goddess to Florida for the best reason of all: Revenge.

A Bride of Salt and Stars

From a secret tomb beneath the ashes of a Mexican volcano, something has broken free. Something luminous. Beautiful. And deadly. From the deepest part of our human legends, she is known simply as The Bride, and she's visiting Florida for dinner, but her arrival has not gone unseen. The Fearless will make certain her reception is memorable.

In a place where creatures like The Bride hunt each night, The Fearless will go to any lengths defending humanity. But only after dark. That's when the hunting is best.

In this battle, new warriors emerge against this timeless evil as Ring, Wally and Risa rejoin their stalwart friends to turn demons into dust — and justice into reality. They're joined by Aurelia, the Romanian stripper who fights better than she dances. Aurelia brings a legendary weapon to bear against The Bride — but first, she'll have to guide Ring through a maze of warlocks, a clever deity, and the ongoing reclamation of the succubus Delphine's soul. Along the way, The Fearless will feed the dog, collect the rent, and act like every day in the sun might be their last.

59422670R00131

Made in the USA
Charleston, SC
03 August 2016